∼FAERIE AFTER∼

By Janni Lee Simner

Thief Eyes

BONES OF FAERIE TRILOGY
Bones of Faerie
Faerie Winter
Faerie After

FAERIE AFTER

BOOK 3 OF THE BONES OF FAERIE TRILOGY

Janni Lee Simner

Random House New York

Visit us on the Web! randomhouse.com/teens

Educators and librarians, for a variety of teaching tools, visit us at
RHTeachersLibrarians.com

Library of Congress Cataloging-in-Publication Data
Simner, Janni Lee.
Faerie after / Janni Lee Simner. — 1st ed.
p. cm.
Sequel to: Faerie winter.
Summary: Liza must journey to the Faerie realm in order to save both worlds from impending doom.
ISBN 978-0-375-87069-9 (trade) — ISBN 978-0-375-97069-6 (lib. bdg.) —
ISBN 978-0-307-97455-6 (ebook) — ISBN 978-0-375-87118-4 (pbk.)
[1. Fairies—Fiction. 2. Magic—Fiction. 3. Coming of age—Fiction.] I. Title.
PZ7.S594Fac 2013 [Fic]—dc23 2012006430

Printed in the United States of America
10 9 8 7 6 5 4 3 2 1

First Edition

To Jane Yolen and Bruce Coville, for encouraging me to write for children and teens at exactly the right time

⤳ Chapter 1 ᘡ

He came to me in the rain, as the first maple leaves were surrendering their green. Beyond the path where I waited, their veins burned orange and red beneath a steel-gray sky, and their branches hissed restlessly as they reached for the falling water. To the other side of the path, the Wall's ivy and hawthorn sighed more quietly as moisture rolled down their yet-green leaves and soaked into their roots. After five months learning the ways of my summoning magic from Karin, I saw without trying the dark shadows within both Wall and trees that were their spirit and life.

More raindrops beaded on my oiled leather cloak. It was Karin who'd heard Matthew's approach as we patrolled the Wall together and who, with a small smile, left me to meet him alone. I couldn't hear Matthew, not over the steady patter of rain, one of many small reminders that, strong though my magic might be, I was human and Karin was not.

Thunder rumbled. A gray wolf rounded a bend in the path, fur soaked and legs streaked with mud. The wolf—Matthew—saw me as I saw him, and he broke into a lope. The shadows within him were as clear as those within the plants, boy and wolf so deeply entwined that I couldn't tell where one ended and the other began. My heart pounded, as if my own shadow, the one shadow I could not see, were trying to push its way past skin and bone to reach him.

I knelt in the mud to draw Matthew into my arms. A wet tongue licked my face as I buried my hands—the right living flesh, the left unmoving stone—in his fur. I breathed the scent of wet wolf and muddy boy, and my contented sigh echoed Matthew's own. Rain trickled beneath my cloak. I didn't care. I wanted to stay here, holding him, forever.

"You came," I said when we drew apart at last. He'd traveled alone, and he'd traveled as a wolf, and unlike the last time he'd done these things, he truly was all right.

I saw a dead oak leaf stuck in his fur. Gray, not brown like most dead leaves, it shivered in my hand when I plucked it free, crumbling to dust and leaving behind a lacework of pale veins. Cold whispered against my fingers. I smelled something stale, like a room closed up too long, and then the veins, too, gave way to dust.

Matthew sniffed the dust on my skin, looked up at me through his quiet wolf's eyes. I saw concern there, but whatever this crumbling leaf meant, it was something that needed words and so would have to wait.

"Mom's all right?" I asked him instead.

Matthew nodded his shaggy head. That question, at least, had a simple answer.

He followed me back to the Wall, where I thrust my good hand into the greenery. It knew me now; branches parted, leaving an open space for us to walk through. I moved my hand to Matthew's back, and together we walked into town. My stone hand weighed me down, but after living with it for five months, I adjusted my balance without thinking.

By the time we reached Allie's house, where I'd been staying, the wind had picked up, turning the corn too wild to harvest and forcing everyone in from the fields. Matthew trotted upstairs to find some clothes, while Allie put water on the fire and her father, Samuel, wrapped a thread of scavenged copper wire around a metal core. The closer and more evenly the coils lay, the better the motor he was trying to build would run. A purple stone glowed on the arm of the couch, casting its cold light on his work.

I was sprinkling tea leaves into empty mugs when I

heard Matthew descend the stairs. I turned as he crossed the room, his fair hair tied back in a damp ponytail, the faded cotton shirt he'd found in Samuel's room stretching across his shoulders, his feet, still specked with mud, bare beneath deerskin pants. My heart started pounding all over again.

"Hey, Liza." Shadows of wolf and boy remained tangled within him, and a stray drop of rainwater trickled down his face. I reached out to brush it away, and then we were holding each other once more, my lips brushing his, his hands making their way into my rain-tangled hair.

Allie cleared her throat beside us. "Can I hug you, too? Or does only Liza get to do that now?"

Matthew and I laughed as we drew apart, and Allie wrapped her arms around him. I saw her shadow and Samuel's as clearly as Matthew's, only there were no animal shapes within them.

"You've gotten taller," Matthew told her.

"Like a beanstalk, Dad says." As usual, Allie's red hair was escaping its braid. "Which makes no sense, because beanstalks grow in all directions, plus they try to strangle you if you wait too long to harvest them."

"Just add it to your list of weird things adults say." Samuel set his spool down on his chair to give Matthew a hug of his own.

The front door opened, and Karin joined us. Her

silver eyes didn't focus on any of us—she'd lost her sight soon after my hand had been turned to stone—but she crossed the room easily enough, her steps silent as all faerie folk's were, her clear braided hair falling down her back. Her shadow was visible to me, too; there was no difference between faerie shadows and human ones.

"And are you well, Matthew?" she asked.

Matthew hesitated. Like everyone with magic, he couldn't say anything that wasn't true; if he wasn't all right, he couldn't pretend he was. "I'm okay," he said at last, as if it were something he'd had to think about, but that on thinking, he'd found true. I reached for his hand and squeezed it, hard.

The water was boiling over. Allie hurried to the hearth to grab the teapot and pour the water into mugs.

"The leaf," I said to Matthew as we moved toward couch and chairs.

"What leaf?" Karin moved to sit cross-legged on the floor.

Samuel returned to his chair, Matthew and I to the couch. Allie shoved mugs into each of our hands, then returned with one of her own. She looked at the space beside Matthew and me, raised her eyebrows, and sprawled out on the floor beside Karin.

"Wait," Karin said. "First, tell me, Matthew. How are Tara and Kaylen?"

"They're fine," Matthew said, not hesitating this time. Tara was my mother, and Kaylen—or Caleb—was Karin's brother.

"And the baby?" Green ivy poked out from beneath Karin's sleeve. Only a plant speaker could wear living plants safely.

"Also fine." Matthew sipped his tea. "Caleb thinks she'll arrive early. Less than a month. I'm to tell you both that if you want to be there for her birth, you should come soon. Within a couple weeks."

"A girl, then," I said. *I had a sister once.* But that seemed long ago, and this child had little to do with that one.

"I get to come, too." Allie glanced at Samuel, who once hadn't been willing to let his daughter anywhere beyond the Wall. "Dad agreed. Healing without a watcher is dangerous at any time, and, well, we all know how far Caleb will go to save Liza's mom." Caleb's magic was for healing, and Allie was his student, just as I was Karin's student, though my magic wasn't as close to hers. "If there are two healers there, Caleb won't be tempted to push too hard, even if something goes—but nothing will go wrong. You know that, right, Liza?"

The tea burned my tongue. No one ever knew nothing would go wrong, not for certain.

"We will hold with all going well," Karin said, as if

she could read my silence. The ivy crept down her arm to wrap around her fingers. "Now, what is this leaf that concerns you?"

"Not just a leaf." Matthew rubbed at the scar around his wrist as he held his mug. "I saw . . . there were places, in the forest, that didn't smell right. Where things had gone all musty and wrong. A leaf I nosed at fell apart at my touch. Other leaves—it was mostly leaves. But also a sapling whose branches were crumbling away on one side, leaving a pile of gray dust." He swallowed. "And a pair of empty boots, as far apart as a man might stand, filled with the same dust."

Allie rubbed her arms. "That's too, too creepy."

Samuel frowned into his untouched mug. I edged closer to Matthew, remembering a shivering leaf, a whisper of cold. "There was a leaf in his fur. It crumbled when I picked it up."

Karin set her tea quietly aside. "Give me your hand, Liza."

The gray leaf hadn't hurt me, not that I could tell. But I put down my mug to set my hand in Karin's. She drew it to her face and held it there with a listening look I'd come to know well. "I smell it still." She let my hand go. I no longer smelled anything, but I couldn't smell as well as Karin, either.

"I do not know what this means." Karin stroked a green ivy leaf. "All I know is that I've caught this scent once before: in Faerie, right after the War."

Once, I believed time fell into two simple parts. There was Before the War with the faerie folk, when few humans knew magic was real, and there was After, when that War had destroyed the human world, and the few who'd survived struggled to stay alive amid the deadly magic the War had left behind, hoping all the while that the faerie folk who'd slaughtered so many of us would never return. I was born After, but not long After, and I grew up in the shadow of the War.

Now it seemed my life held many Befores. Before my father set my baby sister out on a hillside to die for showing signs of magic, and Before I sent him away for it. Before my mother ran away and I found her in Faerie, where I learned that humans had sent killing fire to destroy the faerie folk as well. Before I called a dead seed from a gray place to grow into a tree using my magic, and in so doing called autumn and winter back into my always-green world. Before Karin and I called spring to follow winter through that same tree, a calling that nearly killed us and during which the newborn plants found Karin's eyes and took her sight.

Before I met Karin and Caleb in the first place and

learned not all faerie folk were monsters. Before I met Karin's mother and daughter and learned some faerie folk were monsters after all. It was Karin's mother, the Lady who ruled Faerie, who'd turned my left hand to stone even as she died. Before Mom had become pregnant once more, this time by Caleb, whom she'd loved before the War, and Before I'd come here with Karin to learn more about my magic.

I moved closer to Matthew. He wrapped his fingers around my stone hand, as if it were no different from my living one. *Before the Lady used faerie glamour to force Matthew to do her will, and Before he was nearly trapped as a wolf forever because of it.*

"Liza," Karin said, "what do your visions show of this crumbling?"

"Nothing." I was a seer as well as a summoner, but I'd had far fewer visions the past few weeks. I'd hoped that meant I was gaining control over when they came to me at last, though Karin said it would be some years before I could call visions entirely at will.

A leaf curled around Karin's finger. "Would you be willing to seek those visions for us now?"

"I'll try." I took the mirror Karin had given me from my pocket, pressing the catch against my dead hand to snap the plastic case open. I steadied my breathing as Karin had taught me, and then I looked into silvered glass more perfect than anything humans had craft for now. The glass cast my own reflection back at me, brown hair streaked with clear locks that hadn't been there a year before, dark eyes large in my suntanned face.

"Focus on the future, if you can," Karin said.

I thought of home, and of the ordinary tasks Matthew and I would return to there: gathering firewood, carding wool, tracking and hunting game—silver light flickered in the glass, went out. I knew well enough I wasn't much of a bow hunter anymore, though I'd been practicing with my stone hand all spring and summer. I kept staring at the glass, thinking instead of Mom, the baby, and Caleb, of Kyle, the young animal speaker who also lived with us now. *Home,* I thought. *Show me home.* I'd learned so much during this time away, and home had not always been kind to me, but with each passing month, I yearned all the more to go back there.

The mirror grew bright again, but reluctantly. I stared into that brightness. The images came slowly, as they never had before, hazy and blurred as if viewed through fog—

Matthew and me, Karin and Allie, walking the path to my town—

Me hugging Mom, wrapping my hands around a belly grown large with the baby within—

Matthew's grandmother, Kate, standing with Karin

*beside a larger mirror, one tall enough to step through—
the mirror through which I'd taken Mom out of Faerie
and through which Karin's daughter, Elin, had fled back
into it. "You must break the glass," Karin said. "Now
that we know there are survivors in Faerie, there's no
telling who else might find their way through." "I know,"
Kate told her, "but the mirror saved Matthew and Liza
and Tara. Are we sure this is over? Are we sure it won't
be needed again?" Kate pressed her lips together, as if
unhappy with where that thought led—*

I came out of the vision to find Matthew, Allie, and
Samuel all staring at me. Often someone needed to call
me out of my visions, but this vision had released me on
its own.

"What did you see?" Karin laced her fingers together,
and the ivy vine twined up her other arm.

"Not much." I slipped the mirror back into my
pocket. "All of us reaching my town, me hugging Mom,
you and Kate talking about her mirror."

"That discussion took place before we left Franklin
Falls." Karin frowned. "Tell me, Liza. What is the fur-
thest you've ever seen into the future?"

"No more than a few weeks." My visions had always seemed more concerned with present and past. "I
thought it was because I was new to my magic."

"As had I." Karin rested her chin on her hands. Thin

green tendrils crawled up her neck to weave themselves into her braid. "Yet in all other ways, your power has grown quickly. And once before I have seen visions cling closely to the present, not only for new seers but for all of them, as if any more distant future were too uncertain for their sight to pierce. Only once—just before the War."

I picked up my mug. The tea had grown cold. "The War's over." It had to be over. My world nearly hadn't survived the first time.

"There are many things that could make the future unclear. A war is but one of them." Karin shook her head, and the ivy tendrils scurried out of her hair. "Perhaps I worry needlessly. But I would examine these dead leaves and gray dust for myself. I do not think we should wait two weeks to go to your town. I think we should go as soon as we can."

We left two mornings later, just long enough for Karin to instruct the other plant speaker in her town—Kimi, a friend of Allie who'd come into her magic shortly after I had, and who, like me, was Karin's student—about maintaining the Wall. Samuel almost didn't let Allie leave after all, and only agreed because my vision showed she would, one way or another, and because, he said, he trusted Karin, Matthew, and me to look after her.

"I don't need looking after." Allie wriggled out of his

final hug, just beyond the Wall. "Besides, Liza knows it's usually me saving her anyway."

I adjusted the pack on my shoulders. "Let's hope no one needs saving this time." I wanted to go home, and hold those I cared for close, and know they were all safe. I wanted to no longer fear, deep down, that that was too much to ever hope for.

We set out, Karin and Allie, Matthew and me, into the morning chill. High clouds streaked the predawn gray, promising more rain in a day or so. Karin swept the path in front of us with her staff as she walked; her other hand lay lightly on Allie's arm. Oak and maple leaves grew along the staff's length, along with tendrils of wild grape that stretched on ahead, warning of rises and falls and rocks in the trail. Karin wasn't wholly blind. Her plant-speaking magic still saw the shadows within all plants. Before dawn, those shadows weren't strongly bound within stem and leaf. When a length of kudzu sent its shadow snaking out onto the trail, Karin's gaze focused on it. "*Day comes. Seek rest.*" At her quiet words, the shadow hastily retreated.

As we left the town behind and the path wound deeper into the forest, I released Matthew's hand and slipped in front of Allie and Karin, while Matthew remained behind them. We kept watch as we walked on.

An elm shadow swiped at us from above. "*Go away!*"

I said. The elm's shadow obeyed me almost as swiftly as the kudzu had obeyed Karin. As a summoner, I could command the shadows in all living things, but with less subtlety than Karin's deeper control of plants. There were only plant shadows in the forest today, though. We were not close enough to winter for shadows of the dead to roam these woods.

The gray sky lightened, and the tree shadows settled more firmly within bark and leaf. Living vines and branches still grabbed at us, because no plant was wholly tame since the War, but so long as we kept to the center of the path, those were easy enough to avoid. Color seeped into the world, revealing a green forest broken by patches of fiery red and orange. *Autumn.* This year autumn was coming on its own, a slow change that needed no command from me. I only hoped spring would do the same.

As the sun rose, Matthew and I switched places, because we had less need for my summoning to protect us by day and because even as a human, Matthew had something of his wolf's sense of sight and smell. His ponytail flopped over the top of the pack Samuel had loaned him. Karin slowed a little as the path became more uneven, and for the first time in months, I heard her faint footsteps as she made her way along it.

Allie reached for the sky, as if she could touch it. "I'm not stupid like a year ago, when I ran away to follow you guys. I know how dangerous things can get, but I don't want to ever live only behind the Wall again. I love this world. I do."

Karin used her staff to push a stone from the path. "This world is a good thing to love," she said soberly.

I loved the world better when I could keep an eye on it. I continued watching and listening as we walked on.

Karin slowed her steps. "Ahead of us."

Matthew came to an abrupt halt. "This one wasn't there before." His voice tightened around the words. A squirrel lay by the side of the path, its fluffy tail twitching, its head pillowed on a pile of gray dust.

Just a dying squirrel, I thought, and then I saw what was missing. Its front and back paws. The tip of its nose. Only the thing's shadow was whole. As I moved to Matthew's side, I smelled the same stale scent I had from the leaf, stronger now. My good hand reached for the hilt of the knife I wore, though I saw nothing to fight here.

"It's awful!" Allie's voice rose. "It's—it's not dead. It should be, but it's not!"

Karin gripped her staff. "Tell me what you see."

"A squirrel." I forced my voice to stay steadier than Allie's as I described it to Karin. Matthew knelt beside the creature, carefully not touching it. There was no blood, just that stale gray dust.

The squirrel's tail kept twitching. All at once Allie

darted forward and pressed her hands to its side. There
was a flash of silver light. The squirrel's shadow flickered
and went out, and its fluffy tail fell still.

"Allie!" I grabbed the back of her shirt one-handed
to pull her away. Matthew scrambled to his feet, reaching for Allie's shoulders, looking her over.

Tears streamed down her face. "I had to! It was hurting so much."

"Kaylen has surely taught you not to throw yourself
into any healing without first determining you can do
so safely." Karin extended her staff toward the squirrel, and a green tendril snaked into the dust. The color
began to drain from it. Karin made a harsh sound, and
the tendril fell, half green, half gray, from her staff. The
gray half crumbled into more dust. "This one is newer
than Matthew's leaf, I think."

Allie backed away from the squirrel. We all did. I
thought of the gray leaf caught in Matthew's fur, and I
shivered. I scanned forest and trail but saw nothing that
could have caused this.

Karin turned back to the path. "I suggest we keep
walking."

A mile on I found a half-crumbled sycamore leaf by
the side of the trail. It didn't affect Karin's staff when
she poked at it, so she moved to the sycamore tree beside it, putting her hands to the furrowed brown bark.

"This tree remembers cold. A time when the midday sun wasn't strong enough to warm its leaves. It would rather not remember."

We didn't speak much after that. Matthew found a pile of gray dust where the sapling he'd seen had been, and we all found more crumbling leaves. Always, Karin poked the dust with her staff before questioning the trees around it. Their answers were no clearer than the sycamore's.

"There's more to this than we can see." Karin's staff met a rock, and she stepped around it. "There are hints of it in the air, too, very faint. I've been catching some of them as the wind shifts."

I didn't feel any wind. "You said you smelled this after the War. What did it mean? Was there dust then?"

"With so much burned to ash, who can say?" The ivy vine poked out from beneath Karin's sleeve, retreated again. "But Faerie was sorely wounded, in ways I do not wholly understand. Every root and branch and stone, every person and every animal, felt that wound, which ran deeper than the burning of the fires the humans sent, felt it and cried out even as they died. No plant or animal speaker could hear those cries and remain sane for long. I'm told the very land cried out, though none but my mother could hear it." Something wild flashed across Karin's face and was gone. "That was all some time ago.

This may not be the same thing. We must watch, and listen, and not leap to fear too soon."

As the sun neared midday, the air grew warm. I rolled up my sleeves, fumbling as I hooked stone fingers—my left hand was frozen halfway into a fist—under the wool to get my right sleeve up. Matthew offered to help, but I shook my head. I'd been practicing this, just as I'd been practicing shooting with bow and arrow, every day. If I was making more progress with my clothing than my hunting, I would nonetheless keep at both until I regained the skill I'd lost.

We took dried meat from our packs, remaining watchful as we ate on the trail. The boots Matthew had seen were gone to dust, too, save for a silver buckle that shone in the afternoon sun. A common pattern—perhaps it had belonged to one of the traders who'd begun visiting my town, now that we didn't turn all strangers away.

Dust and crumbling leaves grew less frequent as the sun slid toward the horizon. A cricket chirped, but it held no danger. Crickets remained one insect that preferred to prey on plants, not people. We took a side trail to loop around my town, because Karin wanted to visit the tree I'd called before we went on to Franklin Falls.

The hillside where it stood blazed with color in the evening sun. The tree—a quia tree, cinnamon-barked and red-leafed—rose above orange and yellow brambles of blackberry and sumac. Its leaves were perfectly round, its shadow clearer and sharper than those of the bushes around it. As far as we knew, it was the only quia tree ever to grow outside of Faerie.

Calling spring to the quia tree had nearly sent me forever into a gray place where only dead shadows lived. I'd feared this crumbling and death might somehow also be tied to the tree, and so my fault—but I felt only green life pulling on me as we reached the hillside, green that longed to grow even as the tree prepared for winter's sleep.

Karin's face held that listening look again.

"Do you feel it?" I asked her.

"Oh yes." Karin thrust her staff into the brambles, and they moved aside, opening a path for us. I followed her to the tree, Matthew and Allie trailing behind me.

Karin leaned the staff against it and put her hands to the bark. The tree's branches rustled, as if catching a breeze. "This tree speaks of the gray, and of the green beyond the gray, and of . . . Liza. Hold out your hand."

I did as Karin said. A branch reached down and cool leaves brushed my palm. Something dropped into my hand: six perfectly round brown seeds.

It was the green life within them that I'd felt. I saw the small curled shadow in each seed from which that life came. "They want to be planted," I said.

Karin smiled at that. "As all seeds do." She reached toward me. "May I?"

I poured the seeds into her palm, but the green in them kept pulling on me. Karin held the seeds as gently as one might hold a newborn child. "These seeds know you, Liza, much as their tree does. And they are strong, for all that they are young." A few ivy leaves poked out from beneath Karin's sleeve, and she rubbed them thoughtfully. "The only seeds I've known before with such strength and will to life came from the Realm's First Tree, and that tree has only seeded twice that we know of. The first time was early in our history. I must tell you that story, and soon."

"I already know it," Allie said. In her town, children memorized stories, because they considered storytelling a skill as important as sowing a field or wielding a bow.

"What's the second time they seeded?" I asked, though I feared I already knew.

A wind picked up as the sun touched the horizon. Karin tilted her head, as if it carried some message only she could hear.

"Just before the War," she said.

⌁ *Chapter 2* ⌁

Karin kept the seeds so she could study them further. Her staff she left by the quia tree, because while as a plant speaker she could control the staff's growth easily enough, my town wouldn't want any greenery near where we lived and slept. We'd seen too many killed by the swift-growing plants the War had left behind, plants that too often sought human flesh and blood.

Seeds were easier to hide, though, and Karin hadn't wanted to leave them behind. I felt the green in them all the remaining way into Franklin Falls, a gentle tug that wasn't unpleasant but that never quite went away. Should I plant them? But Karin said that if the seeds were here, they must be here for a reason, and we should first try to puzzle out what it was.

Matthew lived right at the edge of town. We neared

his house as the sun dipped beneath the horizon. I saw Mom on the porch talking with Matthew's grandmother, Kate, and with animal speaker Kyle, who'd turned six while I was away. Their hands and faces were streaked with dirt, no doubt from a day spent bringing in the harvest.

Mom turned at the sound of our steps. She looked well, dark hair tied back, the gauntness gone from her face, her belly large with the child she carried. Kyle retreated behind Kate as I shrugged off my pack and climbed the stairs to wrap my arms around her, clinging as if I were a child as well.

"Lizzy." Mom held me close as she stroked my hair. "I've missed you so much."

My body pressed up against her belly. "You're all right?" Of course she was all right. Matthew had said as much, but it hadn't always been true, and I hadn't known until then how badly I'd needed to see it for myself.

"I'm fine," Mom said as she pulled away. A silver-plated leaf hung from a chain over her stretched-tight sweater. Caleb's quia leaf, from Faerie's First Tree, which held some piece of Caleb's being deep inside it. "The baby's fine, too." Mom's gaze flickered over my stone hand, flickered too quickly away. "You?"

I thought of how she'd nearly died in Faerie, of how

the fire—the *radiation*—in the air there had seeped into her skin and bone. But that was over. For a few heart-beats I allowed myself to believe I truly had saved her, and Matthew, and all those I held dear.

Pieces of the forest were crumbling away. None of us were safe. I forced that thought aside. "I'm good, too," I said, because right here and right now, it was true. I looked at Mom's shadow and saw, faintly, the baby's shadow tangled within it. I touched her stomach gently, wonderingly. The baby hadn't had its own shadow when I'd left. A small shadow fist reached toward me. For an instant, our hands seemed to touch.

I'd keep the baby safe, too, once she was born. I would.

Caleb stepped out of the house, his clear hair fall-ing to his shoulders, his steps silent as he crossed the porch to us. A silver coin hung from his neck, a gift from Mom, though there was no magic in it. "I'll be surprised if she waits more than another couple weeks to join us. She's getting restless in there." I'd never seen Caleb smile like he did when he said that, a smile that reached his silver eyes and held nothing of sorrow in it. He couldn't see shadows, but as a healer, he had his own ways of feeling the life within his daughter.

Allie flung herself at him. "I *missed* you," she told her teacher.

I turned to Kyle, meaning to hug him as well. The boy turned his back to me. I laughed a little and walked around to face him. "Hey, Kyle."

Kyle stalked past me, small shoulders stiff, past Karin, Kate, and Matthew and down the stairs. I'd saved Kyle as well, but he wasn't acting like I'd saved him.

Mom sighed as Matthew and Kate took our packs, set them down on the porch, and headed inside; as Allie let Caleb go, and Karin and Caleb talked quietly. "Kyle missed you, that's all," Mom said.

He didn't look like he missed me. "I came back. Just like I promised." I'd promised Kyle so many things: that I would look after him. That I'd teach him about his magic. But I'd needed to learn more about my own magic first, and Mom had said she'd help me take care of him, freeing me to go with Karin.

Mom leaned against the porch railing. "He didn't understand how long it would be. Five months is forever to a child. He'll be okay. He just needs to be sure of you again."

A yellow kitten padded over to Kyle and nudged his boot. It was the great-grandkitty of my first cat. Kyle knelt beside it and made a low mewling sound, speaking to it as he wouldn't speak to me. "Sorry, Kyle," I whispered. If Kyle heard, he gave no sign. The kitten made a questioning sound, and Kyle picked it up to hug it tightly. When we moved inside, Kyle followed, holding the kitten close.

Kate's living room held a faint purple glow from the lit stones that lay positioned around it, the work of one of the children in our town, who was a stone shaper. There were a couple of orange stones, too, giving heat without smoke. Not everyone in my town was as willing to use magic for light and heat as Kate and Mom were. My town wasn't near as easy with magic as Karin's.

Kate's mirror was nowhere in sight. Matthew had said that while she hadn't been willing to shatter it, she had taken it from the house to store it facedown in the shed, weighed down with rocks so that none could step through it. Somewhere beyond that mirror, did Karin's daughter wonder whether her mother was well, too? It was to save Karin that Elin had helped kill the Lady at last, but before that Elin had destroyed a human town, and afterward she'd fled back to Faerie through the glass rather than talk with her mother. Karin had scarcely spoken of her daughter since.

Other Afters—children born since the War, and so with magic—found their way to Kate's house: object caller Seth with his little sister and brothers; wood shaper Charlotte, holding her cane with one hand and the scarred hand of fire speaker Ethan—whose town it was Elin had destroyed—with the other, though they'd not been a couple when I'd left; wind speaker Hope, with her husband and sister, her own newborn baby held close in a sling.

The baby's shadow was dark and healthy within him. As I took him in my arms, he stared up at me through bright silver eyes. I stared back and ran my hand over his fluff of clear hair. "There hasn't been . . . trouble?" My sister had died for showing such obvious signs of magic.

Hope laughed, shaking the tiny carved acorns at the ends of her braids. In winter Hope wore real acorns, but in summer true seeds could too easily sprout and try to take root in her skin. "Of course there's been trouble. But this baby and me agree on something. We're not going anywhere." She glanced at Mom. "No offense, Tara, but we can't all leave, can we? Where would the younger ones and their magic be then?"

"Leave?" I looked at Mom. She and Caleb and the baby were staying here. They'd decided that before I'd left. "What do you mean, leave?"

Mom looked away. Had she changed her mind while I was gone? I handed the baby back to Hope, and he fussed in his mother's arms.

Hope adjusted her sweater to feed him. "You haven't already told her?"

"Told me *what*?" I'd thought Mom was done keeping secrets from me.

Her hand went to the leaf she wore. "We'll talk later," she said softly.

The kitten stalked away from Matthew and Kyle to sniff at one of the glowing stones. Its nose touched the orange light, and it bolted from the sudden heat, though surely it had met such before. Matthew moved to my side to rub my left shoulder. I sighed and leaned toward him. My shoulder grew tired by day's end from my stone hand's weight. Matthew had taken to rubbing the soreness away.

People kept drifting into Kate's house, Afters and adults both, crowding the living room, full of questions about the journey and about Karin and Caleb's town, Washville. I saw small changes in them as they all spoke: a broken finger, once healed at a bad angle, now grown straight; a child's lost hearing restored; the town blacksmith, walking without a cane. Caleb's work—I wondered what my townsfolk made of that magic. Some stole glances at my dead hand when they thought I wasn't looking. Once, I'd covered my hair to hide the clear streaks there, but now, I was too strongly touched by magic to have any chance of hiding.

We told the townsfolk, in bits and pieces, about the crumbling we'd seen, and their interest in our travels turned to concern. By the time people began drifting away, a Council meeting had been called. Kate passed around bowls of porridge to those who lingered, cooked on more glowing stones in the hearth, and only then did I realize how late it was. I ate hungrily, balancing the bowl in the crook of my left arm as I'd learned to do.

It was even later when the last visitors went home, leaving just Mom and me and Kyle; Matthew and Kate; and Karin, Caleb, and Allie. Kyle curled on the couch with the kitten, the two of them purring at each other.

"Liza and Matthew," Karin said. "In the morning, you must both speak to the Council. I would join you, but I'm too much of a stranger to be welcome there, and I'll not have this danger ignored on account of that." She left unsaid what we all knew: that while being a stranger would cause problems enough, her not being human would most trouble the Council. The townsfolk had stared at her far more openly than me, and though she could not see that, she could hear the whispers as they worked out who she was, though those who were the most uneasy hadn't come at all. I'd see a couple of them at the Council tomorrow.

I wondered how Caleb had managed here as long as he had. How could I blame him and Mom if they were thinking of leaving? It only made sense, more sense than the anger I felt when I thought about it.

"Of course we'll talk to the Council." I set my empty bowl down and slipped outside. Matthew followed. We walked down the porch stairs, around beneath the eaves. The clouds had begun to thicken over the stars, and the wind was picking up, bringing the scent of rain.

Matthew wrapped his arms around me. "What's wrong?"

I leaned my head on his shoulder. "They're thinking of leaving. Mom and Caleb. Did you know?"

"No." Matthew's hold on me tightened. He no more liked Mom keeping secrets than I did. Whatever she and Caleb were thinking, they hadn't talked about it until after he'd left. "You can stay here," Matthew said. "With me and Gram. You know that."

How could I not stay? I imagined the five months Matthew and I had been apart becoming normal, our visits to one another rare islands in a sea of absence. I didn't want that. I pressed my face against his neck, inhaling his wolf-and-boy scent. I imagined my baby sister, growing up a day's walk away, seen only a few times each year, and liked that no better. "I don't know what to do if they go."

I thought of Matthew out in the forest, his nose to a dead gray leaf. The world was crumbling away. Maybe it didn't matter what I decided. I trembled in Matthew's arms, trembled even as his lips found mine. It was a long time before we pulled apart.

I traced a finger along his jaw. The faint fuzz there

was thicker than when I'd left. Matthew stroked the back of my stone hand. I wanted to feel his touch. I reached for him with my living hand, and he stroked it just as gently. A few thin strands had fallen from his ponytail. I blew them from his face, and then somehow we were kissing again, Matthew's hands tangling in my hair as I pushed him up against the house—

A footstep creaked on the porch. Matthew and I scrambled apart to see Allie looking over the railing, watching us with open curiosity. She turned away when we saw her and headed down the stairs. The others followed, Kyle in Caleb's arms, leaning sleepily on his shoulder. The kitten had climbed into the boy's hair. It and Kyle batted lazily at each other.

Mom put a hand on my arm. My sweater was askew, and my face grew hot as I realized I wasn't sure quite when that had happened. "Ready, Liza?"

Matthew squeezed my good hand. My lips brushed his, more briefly, and then I grabbed my pack from the porch and followed Mom home, Caleb and Kyle beside us. Karin and Allie were staying with Kate and Matthew, because they had an extra room and we didn't. My room had been given over to Kyle while I was gone. We'd be sharing it now.

Inside our house, I inhaled familiar smells: fresh-ground cornmeal, the oil of uncarded wool, the faintest hint of smoke from the fire that had burned our house five months before, though all other signs of it were gone. Mom reached for a stone beside the door, hitting it against several other stones around the living room to fill the space with purple light before sinking wearily into a chair. The kitten leaped to the floor and darted up the stairs as I set my pack down beside the couch. Kyle had fallen asleep in Caleb's arms.

"Some days a few extra naps sound pretty good to me, too," Mom said.

"Then you should take them," Caleb said severely. "The harvest will get brought in regardless."

Mom shook her head, dismissing the words. "I'll be little enough use the first few days after she's born. I'm fine, Kaylen."

Caleb's fingers brushed Mom's cheek. He looked at her, and there was something in his gaze—I turned away. My father had never looked at my mother like that.

Caleb carried Kyle up the stairs. The boy shifted in his arms. I looked back at Mom.

"Do we have to talk about it now, or can it wait until morning?" she asked me.

"Are you leaving or not?" I focused on untying my pack one-handed.

Mom took a glowing stone from the couch, set it back down. "I thought you'd be glad to leave," she said, which was good as an answer. "You were so eager to head for Washville with Karinna. You were happy there, weren't you?"

One of the backpack straps had gotten knotted. I took the knot in my teeth as I struggled to get it undone. "I was happy." Karin was a kinder teacher than any I'd known before, and it was a weight lifted to live some-place my magic was fully accepted. "But I always knew I'd come home." The knot wouldn't give. I reached for my knife.

Mom pushed herself out of the chair and took the strap from me, undoing it easily enough with her two good hands. I grabbed it back. I could have managed on my own.

"Kyle will come to Washville, too. His mother's al-ready said she won't try to stop him. This town . . ." Mom eased herself back into the chair. "I know things have gotten better here. But what if they don't stay bet-ter? What if the baby . . ." She wrapped her arms over her stomach, leaving the thought unspoken. We both knew what had happened the last time Mom had given birth to a child with visible magic.

"Hope's baby lives," I said. "Caleb's spent five months here in peace, too."

"Ethan nearly burned the woodshed with his magic last week, after he'd been doing so well at learning control. Did you know that? That spooked lots of folks. There'll always be something to spook someone," Mom said. "I thought I could do this, but it just isn't safe for her here."

The baby's shadow was curled in on itself now, as if asleep. I pulled bags from my pack, setting them out to air. I'd suffered enough for living in this town, and Mom had never tried to find somewhere safer for me.

She let her hands fall to the arms of the chair. "Kaylen's presence here makes folks uncomfortable enough, but he's willing to endure their mistrust for my sake. The baby, though—if things got ugly again, if we failed to protect her—I can't do this anymore, Liza. Five months ago I told myself I could handle it, but I can't."

She struggled back out of the chair. I reached out, too late, to help her. "We won't go anywhere until the baby's born," she said. "You have some time yet."

"I didn't say I was going with you," I told her.

"We'll talk about it." Mom started for the stairs.

I followed her up. There was nothing to talk about. The time when my mother could make my decisions for me was long past.

In my room—what had been my room—Caleb was tucking the blankets in around Kyle. Mom and I watched from the hall.

"How are your nightmares?" she asked me.

"Not so bad." During my months in Washville, they'd grown rarer. Maybe I should be glad to go back.

Caleb joined us in the hall. "Kyle, at least, knows when he needs to rest," he said.

Mom kissed the top of my head, as she hadn't since I was small. "See you in the morning, Lizzy?"

I just nodded. Mom's hand slid into Caleb's, and I watched as they walked down the hall and into Mom's room, feeling strange, though it was no secret they were sharing a bed. They were having a *child* together, after all. As the door closed, I went into my own room. One leg of my dresser had been gnawed halfway through, by the kitten or by some other wild creature of Kyle's, I didn't know. Kyle had sprawled out in sleep, tossing aside the blankets Caleb had so carefully arranged, but there was space enough beside him on the feather mattress. I stepped toward it. The boy opened his eyes, looked up at me, and rolled firmly away. The kitten snuggled in beside him. He gave the kitten a sleepy kiss—or was it a lick?—on top of his head.

"Kyle?"

The boy scooted farther from me, holding the kitten close.

I knew well enough when I wasn't wanted. I sighed and headed back downstairs. Time enough to try to talk to Kyle tomorrow. I pulled off my boots and my socks and my knife in its sheath and curled up, still dressed, in an old comforter on the couch. I was so, so tired, and tomorrow there was the Council to speak to, and the crumbling to think about, and always, the harvest to bring in.

I shut my eyes, but my thoughts jumbled one over another. It took me a long time to find sleep.

What seemed moments later, I woke to a voice I hadn't heard in five months, whispering, "Liza. Come here."

∽ Chapter 3 ∽

I knew that voice. Elin, Karin's daughter. Eyes still closed, I reached for my knife. She would not have come, in secret and in the dark, if she did not mean harm.

"Take no weapons, Liza." Her voice remained soft, like silk from Before. My fingers brushed the sheath but did not grasp it. "Make no sound. Stand."

The words shuddered through me. *Faerie glamour.* I had an instant to feel fear—to open my eyes, to reach for words with which to command Elin away—and then I pressed my lips back together. Elin had said to make no sound. I didn't want to make any sound. I didn't want to do anything to displease her. Silently I stood, leaving the knife behind. I couldn't remember quite why I'd wanted it.

"Very good." Elin was little more than a shadow in the dark. Beneath her cloak her shoulders relaxed, as if she'd been afraid but was no longer. "Come with me. Remember, no noise. You are good at being quiet, aren't you?"

I *was* good at that. Suddenly I wanted, more than anything, to show Elin just how good. I padded across the room and out the door in my bare feet, carefully placing each foot before I lifted the next. Outside, wind blew splatters of cold rain into my face. I walked down the outside stairs, and Elin followed, leaving the door open. Up above, a half-moon struggled to poke through the clouds. I walked by Elin's side, dirt damp beneath my bare toes, hoping my silence pleased her.

Elin stopped at an empty space between two houses. A man I didn't know joined us there. The moon caught the clear thin braids that framed half his delicate face, the fall of loose hair that obscured the other. His tunic was belted with links of dark stone shot through with lighter streaks, and his silver eyes regarded me coldly as he reached for my stone hand. A shiver rippled through it as his living fingers wrapped around my dead ones. My eyes went wide. I'd felt nothing in that hand since the Lady had changed it.

"You may recall," Elin said softly, "that I have vowed

not to harm you or anyone else from your town. Fortunately, Nys here has made no such promises. Should our control over you slip, you might remember that."

Why would I want their control over me to slip? We kept walking, past Kate's house and to the shed behind it with its recently repaired roof. I focused on keeping my steps quiet, on the way Nys's fingers wrapped around mine, though my hand was dead once more. Something leaned against the shed, glinting in the moonlight. Kate's mirror, the one she kept inside that shed so no one could use it. I wondered if Nys and Elin had moved it, and how they'd gotten past the guards my town now set at its borders, but those were distant thoughts, of less interest than the way Nys put his free hand to the glass and the way the glass parted at his touch. Faerie folk were hard enough for humans to hear.

"Follow him," Elin whispered. "While you do, I shall have a talk with my mother."

"Close your eyes." Nys's voice was as quiet as Elin's, but harsher, catching on something inside me the way silk caught on work-worn hands. "I'll not have you altering our destination, little seer."

What destination? I shut my eyes, obeying the command, wanting to please Nys as dearly as I did Elin. He stepped forward, and I followed him. I felt glass part like water around me, felt water thicken into stone. Stone

pressed the air from my chest, and then I burst gasping into the open air. Warm wind caressed my face and
neck. "You may open your eyes again," Nys said.

A half-moon lit the clearing where we stood, just like
the moon at home. But we weren't home, and no clouds
stopped this moon's light from reflecting off the oblong
of shining black stone that stood beside us, as tall and
flat as Kate's mirror and nearly as bright. Nys pulled
me down onto a low bench, made of duller stone, to sit
beside him. Bench and standing stone were surrounded
by a ring of dead trees, little more than burned snags. I
knew where we were, then: Faerie. I'd never been anywhere else with so many dead trees. The largest snag
held a shadow that stretched beyond where the stump
ended, branches grasping like arms at the sky, but all
the others were as dead within as without. Dark ash lit-
tered the ground, and the air held a faint stale scent, a
troubling scent.

Nys turned my head toward him. "So you're Liza."
He took my hand in his again. His fingers ran over the
stone, and I felt their touch deep within it. Thoughts of
why the stale scent should concern me faded. I leaned
toward Nys, reaching for his face with my good hand.
Beneath the fall of loose hair, his skin felt rough and
furrowed.

Nys pushed me away. "I am past playing games with

humans, save when it serves some greater purpose. This glamour is a tool for holding you here, nothing more. Elin wishes to bring her mother home and believes your presence the most effective way to compel her to come. She thinks Karinna might know some way we do not to slow the Realm's steady crumbling, and so I have pledged my support. You made it easy for us, sleeping by the door. We were prepared to work much harder to get to you. As it was, we needed only to locate the mirror, an easy enough task, if one that required some walking."

Nys stroked my hand once more. It tingled with life. His fingers crept past the sensitive spot at my wrist to touch living skin. Something rose in me at that touch. I moved closer to him as his fingers strayed back to the stone, feeling his warm breath against my face. Again Nys pushed me away. What had I done to displease him so?

He dropped my hand and stood. The shining stone rippled, and Elin stepped through it. Karin followed, her hand on Elin's arm, her stance watchful.

Allie followed Karin, fingers clutching the plant speaker's sweater. "Of course I won't leave you!" Allie cried. She fell silent as the warm wind blew her night-gown about her ankles. "Oh." Allie bit her lip and looked around, as if taking the whole of ruined Faerie in.

I stood, too, reaching for Nys with my stone hand

as I sidled closer to him. Allie's eyes went wide, but I couldn't work out why, any more than I could work out the strange green tug I felt from where Karin stood.

"Where is Liza?" Karin drew away from Elin and reached for Allie, who took her hand.

"I'm here." Surely Karin heard my steps and breath, just as always.

"Come to me, Liza." Karin's voice was tight. Angry, as I rarely heard it.

Nys took my stone hand back in his. *Yes. This.* "Can't," I told Karin, a little breathlessly. *Don't want to.*

"Let Liza go." Karin's other hand was clenched at her side. "Release her from your glamour, and allow them both to return to their own world. Only then will we talk."

"I think not." Elin's dress rippled where it brushed the ground, as if alive. Her magic was for weaving. "You refused to return to *this* world after the War that nearly destroyed us, for my sake or your people's sake. If holding your student's leash is all that prevents you from taking flight once more, I shall hold it."

"I cannot stay here." Karin held herself so stiffly, with none of her usual easy stillness. "Let them go, and then I will explain. If you acknowledge Liza is my student, you acknowledge, too, that she is not yours to hold."

"There are greater bonds than that between student

and teacher." Elin dropped to her knees, but her eyes remained defiant. "Such as the bond between the Realm's own ruler and her people." Nys knelt, too, pulling me to the ground beside him.

"The land is unraveling, and we have need of your knowledge and your power." There was ice in Elin's voice. "Does that not matter to you more than a couple of mere humans? Or do you care so little for your own true people that you would release your claim on us?"

"The land." Karin held tight to Allie's hand as she spoke. "You cannot imagine what the land says to me. It is worse, so much worse than before, when my mother yet lived and it was only the plants I heard. I cannot hold out for long. I thought I'd have more time. Daughter, please. Return with us to the human world and we will talk. You have my word."

"No," Elin said. "You will not choose humans over me, not this time. If you wish to speak, speak here."

"I must know Liza is unharmed first." There was something unsteady—something *wrong*—in Karin's voice. "I cannot see her, as you well know. She must come to me."

Karin had never asked for anything on account of her lost sight before, any more than I'd asked for anything on account of my dead hand. *Not dead.* Faintly I felt Nys's fingers wrapped around mine. He looked at Elin.

Elin pressed her lips together and nodded. They both rose, and Nys released my hand. "Go to your teacher, Liza."

I didn't want to leave him, but I wanted less to disobey him. I walked to Karin's side, saw fear in her silver eyes. I'd seen Karin concerned, cautious, but never afraid. "I'm all right. Truly." I let her take my good hand in hers.

She pressed something into that hand. Seeds. The green tugging grew stronger, and I knew it for what it was: the call of seeds that wished to grow. For a moment more I longed to return to Nys's side, but the seeds' pull on me was stronger than Nys's was. His glamour melted away like fog beneath sun.

My stomach churned as I clutched Karin's hand. An instant before, I'd wanted nothing more than to touch Nys, to be near him. Now I was sharply aware my knife did not hang by my side, for if it did, I'd have plunged it through his heart. The things he'd made me feel, when he'd touched my hand—

I had no need of a knife to defend myself. "*Go away, Nys!*" I threw my summoning magic into that call.

Nys frowned, but he remained where he was, and I knew that wasn't his full name. Karin and Caleb were the only faerie folk I'd met who gave their full names to humans, a sign of trust and respect I'd not understood at first. Most faerie folk were cautious about sharing their true names with any but those nearest them, even among their own people.

I swallowed panic down like bitter willow bark. I dared not let the fear that followed glamour weaken me. I drew my hand from Karin's, keeping the seeds out of view as I slid them into my pocket, beside the mirror.

The ivy leaves at Karin's wrist were wilting, one by one. "The land knows me, now that the Lady is gone. I cannot fight it—you and Allie must leave this place."

"We won't go without you!" Allie said as Karin pressed her hand toward mine and I took it. I'd been thinking the same thing. If something needed fighting, we'd help Karin fight it.

"Liza, please." Karin's voice held steady, but there was something in her eyes, beyond their lack of focus, something wild seeking to break free. Whatever she fought, it was somewhere inside her. "I will not leave until I know you are both safe."

Of course we wouldn't abandon Karin here. I looked to the standing stone. It grew bright, catching the moon's silver glow. I stepped toward it, seeking the seer's visions that would lead us safely home.

"Oh, I think not." Nys touched the stone an instant before I did, and as he did, I saw—

Matthew, running toward Kate's mirror, his grand-mother right behind. The silvered glass shattered, send-ing shards flying. Matthew threw up his arms, mouthed my name—and then the image shattered as the glass had, and I stared at lifeless stone.

Nys gave me a dark look. "So you see. Stone shaping and visions go together nearly as well as summoning and visions do. Come here, Liza."

The glamour in his voice was a velvet rope, pulling me toward him. The seeds' pull remained stronger. I backed away, clutching Allie's hand. She grabbed Karin's hand in turn. Karin made whispering sounds as she rocked back and forth on her heels. Elin stepped toward her mother, looking uncertain for the first time.

"There are many ways to control humans." A rough smile crossed Nys's face. "Allie. Come to me, please."

It wasn't her full name, but for glamour, unlike sum-moning, it was enough. Allie stiffened and jerked free of my grasp. She dropped Karin's hand and started toward Nys, feet shuffling through the ash as if she were asleep. I grabbed Allie's hand again; she barely seemed to notice.

Karin fell to her knees. "This is not right. This can-not last. Too long has death been held back—the seeds are not enough. Roots crumble, branches fall—*run!*" Karin toppled forward into the ashes. Elin ran to her side as Allie reached for Nys's cheek, a slow, fascinated smile crossing her face.

Karin began shuddering where she lay. Elin grabbed her shoulders and rolled her over. "Don't you dare," she hissed. "Don't you dare leave me again."

Allie lurched free and threw herself toward Nys. I grabbed her before the stone shaper could. Elin wouldn't let her mother die if she could help it, but no one here cared what happened to Allie but me.

Karin's voice rattled like wind through dry branches, nothing human in it. Allie twisted in my hold. I couldn't protect them both, and I couldn't fight Nys and possibly Elin while doing so.

Nys kept smiling, and I knew he knew it, too. "Allie, child. Come here."

"Sorry, Karin." I threw Allie over my shoulder, and I ran. My feet crunched over dead ash, kicking up clouds of dust. I'd come back. Somehow, I'd come back. Allie wriggled and pummeled my back and kicked my shins. "Let me go! I have to go to him!"

I didn't waste breath to glance back to see whether Nys followed. I put all my energy into running, weaving around more dead tree snags and ignoring the small rocks that cut my bare feet. The warm wind stole the moisture from my throat.

Allie went limp over my shoulder. "Don't let me go," she whispered. "Please."

"I won't." I ran faster without her fighting me. Ash gave way to smoother stone.

The ground shuddered, and emptiness gaped open beneath me. Allie screamed as we tumbled into the dark.

I didn't let go, not even when I crashed into more stone with a sharp snap. *Like bone breaking,* I thought, and then pain seared through my leg and hip.

Just like that. The pain roared into a fire, burning all other thoughts away.

⌐ *Chapter 4* ⌐

I fought to breathe through the burning, to see, to move.

"Hold still!" Allie cried. Numbing cold melted the fire away. I tried to sit up, and pain flared hot once more. Allie pushed me down onto my back. "I mean it!" Her hands moved along my body, lingering over my right hip and leg.

My eyes were closed. I opened them. The dark remained thick as before. Light shimmered, faint and silver, gone before I could focus on it. Pain gave way to an icy pins-and-needles feeling that was intensely . . . uncomfortable. I let out a breath. I could handle uncomfortable.

"That's better," Allie said. "I'm"—she laughed— "working in the dark, you might say. That's okay. It's not like I feel broken bones with my eyes. Here—" Her hands glowed with silver light, stronger than the shimmer I'd seen before. By that light I saw her pale, pinched face. "Oh!" A half grin broke through the worry as her hands flared brighter. "Well, that's better, then."

Cold pulsed through my hip and leg. There was another jolt of pain. I hissed through clenched teeth, and then more cold took the pain away. I felt bones knitting together, itchy under my skin, and reached out to scratch at them without thinking. Allie slapped my hand away. Itchiness gave way to a dull ache, and the light flickered and went out. In the darkness left behind, I saw a faint gray shadow: Allie's shadow, visible to me even in the dark, where nothing else was.

"Sorry, Liza." Allie's voice broke on a sob, and her shadow arm brushed across her shadow face. "Even magic can't stop setting a bone from hurting like anything."

"I'm okay." I reached for her, but Allie pulled away. "Stop moving! The bones need time to get used to being healed so they don't break all over again." She ran her hands over the rest of my body, stopping at my feet. Light flared again as she healed the small cuts on my soles. We were in a small round stone room with no visible doors and a high ceiling that showed no signs of the hole we must have fallen through.

"We're trapped." Allie's voice, as the light faded, sounded terribly young.

I wanted to tell her everything was all right, but no one with magic could lie. "Can you keep your hands lit?" We needed to know if there was any way out of here.

"That only works when I'm healing, and there's nothing left to heal. I'd have to—I mean, I could hurt you so you'd need healing, but I'd never do that! You know I wouldn't." Her voice took on a stubborn edge. "I'd rather stay in the dark."

I knew Allie well enough to also know there was no point telling her I'd willingly endure some extra scrapes and bruises if they'd help us see our way free. "You're sure I can't stand yet?"

"I wouldn't say so if it wasn't true," Allie said severely.

"All right. I need you to feel your way all along the wall for both of us, then. If there are any cracks, anything that might be a door, any handholds we can climb to examine the ceiling, anything that might lead to a way out, we need to know about it."

"Right. So we can get back to Karin." Allie's steps shuffled away from me.

I didn't want Allie anywhere near Elin and Nys. I wanted to get her safely out of Faerie and go back for Karin without her. I watched as her shadow moved around the room, thinking of how Karin walked steadily through the dark, day after day.

With the ache in my hip fading, my thoughts had room to circle back to the way Karin had fallen, the way she'd lain shuddering on the ground—the way I had left her. *You cannot imagine what the land says.* What had Karin heard? Maybe Caleb would understand what had happened to her. Glamour wouldn't touch him if he came back with me.

"Liza? I don't feel anything. It's perfectly smooth, all the way round."

"All right." I didn't know any stone that formed itself into a perfectly smooth cave, not without magic. Nys's stone shaping? Allie returned to sit cross-legged by my side. It was likely Nys who'd made the stone give way beneath our feet and who kept us trapped here now. The chances of either of us getting out of Faerie were pretty small. I brought my left hand to my face, shuddering at the memory of how Nys had brought feeling to the dead stone. I'd been as defenseless against Nys's glamour as Allie, until Karin gave me those seeds.

I fumbled through my pocket, around the plastic mirror case, now cracked, to find the seeds. Five of them—Karin had kept the last for herself. I drew one from my pocket, saw the small shadow curled within it.

"Stay still!" Allie protested, but this time I ignored her to put the seed into her hand.

Allie's fingers closed around it. "Protection? Like Caleb's leaf? Is that why you were able to run?"

"I don't know if it'll work for you," I said. Allie was neither a plant speaker nor a summoner. She wouldn't feel the life in the seed like Karin and I did.

"But it might?" Allie said.

"It might."

Allie slid the seed into what must have been her pocket before she sidled up beside me. "You're shivering, Liza."

It was cold underground. I hadn't noticed. I sat up to put an arm around Allie, and this time she didn't stop me. "You're shivering, too," I said.

"I know. I—" Allie's voice caught, steadied. "What Nys did to me. That was glamour?"

"Yes." My eyes searched the dark. I knew I wouldn't hear Nys, or Elin, or any of the faerie folk coming, but I could see them as I saw Allie.

"When he called me. The things I felt—the things I wanted . . ." Allie hunched over.

"I know." I smoothed her tangled hair.

"No one should have magic like that," Allie said fiercely. "Or if they have it, they shouldn't use it. I can't believe Caleb and Karin ever used glamour, not even during the War, no matter what they say. Karin." Allie drew a troubled breath. "Do you think she's all right?"

"I don't know." The look in Karin's eyes, the sounds she'd made . . . *It is worse, so much worse than before,* she'd said. *Roots crumble, branches fall.* I thought of clouds of ash and dust, of the stale scent in the air, of Karin saying she'd met that scent before, after the War. *It meant the land was gravely wounded.* What if the War and Faerie were where the crumbling began? What if humans did worse than burn people and trees when they sent their fire? I drew the mirror from my pocket. The glass within the broken case felt cracked as well. In the dark, it offered up no visions. I pried loose the largest shard I could find. A weak weapon, but I had none better.

"I *can* feel it," Allie said abruptly.

"Feel what?"

"The seed. It's only a whisper, but there's something in there. Something that has to do with my magic. That makes no sense. My magic isn't for plants, only people and animals. But there's a whisper of something human here. Like a memory."

"That's good." Maybe the seed would protect her after all. "Keep it safe."

"I will," Allie said soberly. "I can feel other things, too. You need to know that. Remember the sickness in the air? The last time we were in Faerie?"

"Radiation poisoning." Even if they weren't responsible for the crumbling, the fires my people sent did harm enough. Their poison remained in Faerie's air long after the War was through, just as blood-seeking trees and raptors with poison in their claws remained in my world.

"It's better belowground than above, but it's down here, too. The air is all wrong—I don't know how the faerie folk have survived so long. They really are harder to hurt than we are. We won't survive anywhere near that long, not unless—" Allie sighed. "We're in an awful lot of trouble, aren't we, Liza?"

My eyes still hadn't adjusted to the dark. I'd never met darkness this deep. "I'll do all I can to protect you."

"I'll protect you, too," Allie said. "I'm still your healer, and I'm not a little kid anymore. I'll do everything I can."

Radiation poisoning was much more dangerous to heal than a broken leg. "Don't do anything that puts you in danger. Promise?"

"I'll promise if you will." Allie laughed a little, but then she sighed again. "Everything's dangerous here, isn't it?"

Very close, Nys's voice answered, "Indeed."

I scrambled to my feet, putting myself between Allie and that voice, ignoring the dull ache that returned to my hip. I saw no shadow to tell where Nys stood. "Show yourself." I reached toward the voice, and my knuckles brushed smooth stone that hadn't been there before.

Rough laughter then. The stone melted away, and a shadow appeared before me. I lunged at it, mirror shard in my hand, aiming for what I hoped were Nys's eyes. I missed, and the glass grazed skin before breaking in my hold.

Nys's fingers closed around my other hand, my stone hand. Fingers that hadn't moved for five months wrapped obediently around his, and warmth tingled through my palm. I wanted to throw up. I focused instead on aiming my knee between Nys's legs.

Nys grunted, but that didn't stop him from dragging me across the room to press my hand to the stone wall. Tingling gave way to white-hot pain, like broken glass being ground into my skin and blood. Fractured bones were nothing compared to this. I fought to pull free, but my hand was gone, melted into the stone. A low animal whimper escaped my lips.

Allie's shadow darted up beside me. Her cool touch took the pain away and cast silver light around the room, showing where Nys stood before me, still holding my arm, blood trickling down his cheek.

"No, Allie." Nys's laughter had given way to anger cold as falling ice. "You will not waste your healing, not on her. Leave Liza be."

Allie stiffened, and I knew there was glamour in his command. Her hand fell to her side, and the light went out.

Pain and fear rose in me, like a river near its banks. I fought them and grabbed Allie's arm. I couldn't let Nys's glamour take her again.

"Let Liza go!" Somehow, Allie's voice remained her own. "You're hurting her!"

"I assure you that is not my intention. But if glamour does not touch Liza, I'll do what I must to control her so that you and I may speak. It appears there are some things Elin has neglected to tell me about you, Allie."

My fingers dug into Allie's nightgown sleeve. "What do you want with us?" I demanded.

"With you, Liza, very little. It is the healer who concerns me." Nys's voice grew thick with glamour. "Come here, Allie. My people have great need of healers."

Allie fought my hold again, struggling to obey Nys's words. Her voice was her own; nothing else was. The seed protected her, but not all the way.

The ground buckled. My feet slid out from beneath me, sending new pain knifing through my arm as it took my weight.

Allie's hand jerked away as I found my footing. Her shadow moved toward Nys. I grabbed for her, but they stepped out of reach.

"Stop it!" Allie said. "Of course I'll heal, if someone's hurt. That's what I *do*. Just let me go on my own. Please." The last word came out quieter than the rest.

Nys took Allie's hand. "I'm sorry, Healer. I do not know why glamour leaves your thoughts free, but I dare not leave any human unbound. We learned, too well, the cost of letting humans run free during the Uprising. I will do what I must to help my people."

"Go away, Nys!" I screamed with all the force of my magic, knowing it wouldn't work, knowing I didn't have his full name, because magic was all I had and I couldn't let Allie go.

Nys sighed, as if I wearied him. "Karinna the Fierce may have worn her name openly in the Realm as a show of courage, but most of us are not so foolish. You are already a problem, Liza. I do not know how it is that you have pulled free of glamour entirely, but you might want to see to it that you do not create further difficulties. I do not need glamour to control you, as you have seen. Come, Allie."

Allie raised her head as she followed Nys across the room, her steps wooden. "You need to know," she said. "I would do this anyway. Hurting Liza and taking me over doesn't change that. Those are your decisions, not mine." Her steps remained steady as they walked away, until stone must have flowed between us once more, because all at once they were gone.

I'd lost her. Panic threatened at the edges of my thoughts. Nys could make Allie do anything now, anything at all. I had to go after her. I had to get away. I felt along the wall, to where my wrist melted into the stone. There were no cracks around it, no way of prying myself free. Flesh flowed smoothly into flat rock, as if they had always been joined. I grabbed my wrist and pulled as hard as I could. Fire roared through the hand I could not see, stealing my breath, making my feet give way. The panic slid up a notch. I fought the stone that held me, fought without thought, knowing only that I had to be free, no matter the pain, no matter *anything*.

No. Beneath pain and fear, a small part of me remembered I could not afford panic now. I forced myself to stop fighting, and I listened for the ragged thread of my breath, remembering Karin's lessons. Breathe in. Breathe out. Again. And again. My breath steadied. The pain and the fear didn't go away, but they no longer controlled me. I kept breathing, counting out the time. Ten breaths. A hundred. I might yet have a chance to save both Allie and myself, but only if I kept my thoughts clear.

I tested the limit of my good hand's reach, feeling

every bit of wall and floor I could get to. The stone was smooth all around. I snapped my mirror open against my hip, taking the plastic case in my teeth to feel for more shards of glass. My fingers traced a spiderweb of cracks, none of the shards among them large enough to serve as a weapon.

Five hundred breaths. A thousand. Light flickered at the edge of my sight. I turned as far as my hand would allow. The light came from a glowing purple stone, carried by a boy with clear hair tangled as willow branches, approaching through a stone tunnel that hadn't been there before.

My broken mirror caught the boy's light. It flashed bright into my eyes, and in that flash I saw—

Mom clutching Caleb's hands. "I've birthed children without magic before," she said. "I can do it again. What I can't do is walk far enough or fast enough—find them, Kaylen. Bring my daughter home—"

Caleb running through a storm-tossed forest, Matthew a wolf at his side. The sky was bruised gray-green, and wind lashed at branches that hissed as rain flew from their leaves. Caleb stopped to put his hands to the surface of a rippling lake. "It is no good. The wind is too strong. We must continue on, toward the Arch—"

A woman I did not know, a faerie woman with bright eyes and a long twisting braid that brushed the

*ground behind her, also running, through forests I did
not know. A ragweed vine lashed out to block her way.
She stopped to give it a long, wry look, and the vine
drew back, letting her pass—*

The vision faded as a voice shouted, "No yelling!"

I jerked at the sound, pulling on my trapped hand,
dropping the mirror. The tangle-haired boy grabbed my
face. His silver eyes glared at me. "I said no yelling!"
His glowing stone lay on the floor, filling the room with
purple light. Across from us, a tunnel stretched into the
distance, if only I could reach it.

I focused on the boy, who, like Elin, looked the same
age as me but was probably older. His sleeves were torn,
and angry red scars ran along his arms. There was something wild in his eyes—it reminded me of what I'd seen
in Karin's eyes, before she'd collapsed. "I wasn't yelling."
I spoke gently, as to a trapped animal.

"Not you." He released my face to grope at my
pocket. *"Them."*

I pushed his hand away, moving my arm to shield
pocket and seeds. Those seeds were all that kept him
from being able to glamour my thoughts away.

"Why so loud? Why so green?" The boy snarled, as
if he were a wild animal in truth, and lunged at me.

I hooked my leg behind his ankle, sweeping him to
the ground. Heat tore through my stone hand. The light

showed, too clearly, the way my wrist melted into the wall.

The boy looked up from where he landed, sniffling like a hurt child. "There is no green," he whined. "There is no loud. There are only gray whispers, whispers that slide between skin and thought, make people say you're crazy. Not crazy. *Not*. The Realm crumbles. No one stops it. Why?"

"I don't know why." I watched, waiting for him to attack again.

The boy began to weep, with a low moaning sound like plants when rain soaked into their roots. He ran his fingers along his arms, nails digging deep, drawing blood.

"What's your name?" I asked, not expecting him to give it, knowing I needed to try for any weapon within reach.

"Tolven." He looked up, and his eyes narrowed, as if suspecting some trick. "You are human. Humans sent the fire. Humans killed the trees. They screamed when they died, so loud—they scream no longer. They whisper of wilting and death." Soft, wet wind sounds wove in around his moaning. The only people I'd ever heard talk in the language of trees were plant speakers. Tolven stood, held out his hands. They were streaked with blood and soil.

Before I could test the name he'd given me, another light lit the tunnel. Nys strode toward us, one of the stone links of his belt glowing. Allie followed at his side, a water skin slung over her shoulder. The girl's steps were stiff, the command that moved them clear, but her eyes were defiant. She flashed me a tired smile, and I let out a shaky breath. She didn't appear to have been harmed.

Nys's sharp gaze fixed on Tolven. He strode forward, grabbed Tolven's shoulders, and turned the boy to face him. "If you have hurt him in any way, Liza, there will be no further kindness from me."

"You've shown us nothing of kindness so far," I said. By the light, I could see scars beneath Nys's loose hair, as if the left side of his face were wax held too near the fire. I'd known humans enough with burn scars, but on Nys's delicate features it seemed more wrong, like cracks in the crystal from Before that was meant to be perfect.

"Whispering hurts," Tolven whimpered. He pressed his hands over his ears, buried his head against Nys's shoulder.

"Hush, child." Nys's voice was low, soothing. More scarred skin showed at the sleeve of his tunic.

"Where's Elin?" Tolven's arms bled, staining his tattered sleeves. "I want Elin."

"Elin remains above. She will return when she may. Come." The stone shaper guided Tolven to the mouth

of the tunnel, stopping to look back at me. "Allie's healing has been of much use to us today." Nys touched the
wall. Ice gripped my trapped hand, and then I stumbled
forward, the hand free, clenched back into its half-fist.
Numbness faded, leaving behind a dull, throbbing ache.

"I know more of kindness than any human who has
not witnessed a world's dying can understand." Nys's
voice was cold. "I leave you with drink. If the healer continues to cooperate, I will bring food as well." He turned
to lead Tolven away.

That tunnel was our only way out—too late, I
grabbed Allie's hand to run after them. Stone descended
like a liquid curtain between us. I pounded it with my
good hand, but the stone held, leaving Allie and me
trapped once more.

⌒ *Chapter 5* ⌒

Allie laced her fingers together, pulled them apart, and laced them together again, as if to prove she could move of her own will. Together, apart, together, apart—she couldn't seem to stop. I grabbed one of her wrists, stilling it.

She looked up at me, brown eyes wide. "I'm all right. Nys didn't make me do anything I wouldn't have done without him. He only made me heal."

Tolven's purple stone lit our prison. Would Nys call that kindness, too? "It's not okay. Nys had no right—"

"Stop!" Allie wore boots beneath her nightgown now, and a cloak over it, both too big for her. "It's bad enough, what he did. Don't make it worse by reminding me how bad. Don't." Allie took the water skin from her shoulder, eyes as intent upon the movement of her arm as they'd been upon her fingers, and offered it to me.

The drink within was fruity and alcoholic. Wine, I realized, though I'd rarely tasted it and was more familiar with my town's medicinal whiskey. Only a plant speaker could grow the fruit for wine safely. The liquid, which was clearly watered down, soothed my parched throat. The air was so dry, even underground. I looked at Allie. She looked away. This wasn't all right, no matter what she thought.

I gave the skin back to her. "We should search the room again, while we have light." We paced the room together but found nothing that might lead to a way out. At last I sat with my back to the wall. Allie set the glowing stone and wine skin in front of us before she sank wearily down beside me.

I kept my dead hand carefully in my lap. I wouldn't let Nys melt it again. "You need sleep after a healing," I told Allie. "I'll keep watch."

Allie laced her fingers back together, stopped herself, and pressed her hands firmly against her thighs. "The healing isn't done. Nys will be back. I don't want him taking me over again while I sleep."

"I won't—" I couldn't promise to stop Nys from using glamour again. I was no more able to protect Allie now than I'd been with my hand stuck in the wall. Helplessness and anger brought a sour taste to my mouth. "Allie, what did Nys make you heal?" A faint hope: might he let us go, when the healing was through?

Allie twisted a lock of loose hair around her fingers. "What do you think?"

"Radiation poisoning?"

"They call it fire fever here. There's so much of it. I only had the strength for two patients—the worst of them—though there were more than a dozen in the room. It's a good thing Caleb taught me a little about how to heal fire fever after he saved your mom. It's so much trickier than other healings. A year ago I couldn't have done it."

"Why can't their healers do it?" They'd have more experience than Allie.

"I don't think the faerie folk have any more healers. Maybe they all died in the War. I hope they all died during the War, because if they didn't, they probably died healing afterward. That would be bad." She twisted her hair tighter and tighter. "I'm not stupid, you know. I understand how important rest is, but I don't think I can sleep, and even if I do, sleep will be worse than staying awake, because if I dream . . ."

"Maybe you'll dream of home." If Nys were here

right now, I'd go for his eyes again, no matter the risk. If he was going to hurt someone, he should have hurt me. I felt the green seeds in my pocket, protecting me still. What use were they, if I was the only one they protected? Surely the quia tree hadn't given me seeds just for that.

The only seeds I've known before with such strength and will to life came from the Realm's First Tree. Karin's words—but if I worried about Karin now, too, I might crumble away beneath the knowledge of all those I couldn't keep safe. *I must tell you that story, and soon,* Karin had said.

Allie had twisted her hair around her fingers, so tightly the skin turned white around it. I put my hand over both of hers, stopping her. She looked up at me, asking for—what?

"You know Karin's story," I said abruptly. "The one about the First Tree and the quia seeds."

"Well, sure, but—"

"Could you tell it to me?" Maybe telling the story would take Allie away from this place, at least for a little while, the way Mom's stories once did for me. If I couldn't take her out of here entirely, I could do that much.

"Now?" Allie narrowed her eyes suspiciously. "You're trying to distract me, aren't you?"

"Yes." I unwrapped her hair from around her fingers. "But I want the story, too. Anything we know about the seeds might help later."

Allie rubbed her fingers where the hair had dug in. "I can't tell it as well as Karin or Caleb."

"That's okay. Just tell it as best you can."

"All right. I remember how Karin started it, at least." Allie tugged the ribbon from what remained of her ragged braid. "She said the story was from when Faerie was new, and the human world that would follow little more than a dream. Dad says that can't be right, because humans have been around for hundreds of thousands of years and Faerie isn't older than that, but Karin says there are many ways of measuring time. It doesn't matter. What matters is that when the story happened, magic was way stronger than today."

Allie's words echoed a little in the stone room. "Shifters could choose any shape. Speakers understood plants and animals and fire and wind all together. And summoners . . ." Allie looked up at me. The purple light gave the circles under her eyes a bruised look. "Summoners weren't limited to calling the shadows in other living things. They could control their own shadows as well, sending them wandering outside their bodies even while they were alive.

"But Karin says not everything was better in those

days, because while faerie magic was stronger, their bodies were weaker. Faeries didn't live much longer than humans, and all sorts of things could kill them too soon." Allie shuddered. "They were so sick, Liza. The people Nys made me heal. All he had to do was ask. Of course I would have healed them." Allie stared at her hands. "It was hard not to keep trying to fight his glamour, inside at least, but fighting didn't work. It only made it worse."

"The story," I said gently.

"The story." Allie worked the tangles from her hair as she spoke. "The story begins with a summoner—Rhianne was her name—who could control her own shadow. And it begins with a speaker, but I don't remember his name. The speaker and the summoner were deeply in love. Of course they were, because that's how these stories go. Together they walked the forests of Faerie, the summoner calling the things of that world to them, the speaker listening to their voices and telling her what they said. But they were too easily distracted by each other's words and presence." A small grin tugged at Allie's face, the first I'd seen since she returned. "That means kissing. You know that, right, Liza?"

"Yes, Allie." I kept my voice as grave as I could manage. "I do know that." I suspected it was far more than kissing Karin meant.

"You *would*," Allie said. "You and Matthew both."

I gave Allie a level look. Her cheeks flushed. We both laughed, but my laughter stopped as I thought of Matthew and Caleb, running through wind and rain to reach us. I would have told Allie about that vision, but what if Nys was listening again?

"So one day while Rhianne and the speaker were *distracted*"—Allie gave me a meaningful look—"a hunting cat saw them. Hunting cats were much bigger than they are now, and this cat's claws swiftly found the speaker's heart. I hate this part. Because while Rhianne used her summoning to send the wild creature away, she wasn't fast enough. The speaker's heart and breath stopped, so fast neither the summoner nor any of Faerie's healers could bring him back, because even then magic wasn't always enough, no matter how strong it was."

Allie tugged a particularly stubborn tangle. "Rhianne's grief at losing her speaker ran so deep. The summoner stopped talking, nearly stopped eating. Months and months later she had a daughter, and once her daughter was born, she decided she was done with life and love and with *everything*, which is the saddest thing I ever heard. Rhianne left her daughter and her people and her body behind, and she sent her shadow wandering, which was stupid, because that meant she was all alone with her grief. Rhianne wandered far and wide, through all of Faerie, while her people waited and watched over her body and hoped maybe one day she'd come back."

The tangle wouldn't give. Allie let it go. "Eventually Rhianne's body grew old and died, because faerie folk died younger then, like I said. Her flesh melted into the soil, and the tree, well, the tree ate her, like trees did, even Before. It was only after that that Rhianne's shadow returned, her grief used up at last. She searched for her body with her magic but found only the tree. And—this is the strangest part. Rhianne sent her shadow into the only shelter she could find for it, the tree's bark and branches and leaves. The tree didn't fight her. Maybe it couldn't, or maybe it recognized her, after eating her skin and bones and all. Karin thinks it welcomed her. No one knows, because this was so long ago. All we know is that Rhianne's shadow and the quia tree's shadow became all jumbled together, and no one could tell, after that, where the woman ended and the tree began. They were the same." Allie leaned against me. "I'm not sure what that means, Liza. Are you?"

I thought of Matthew, wolf and boy at once. "I think it means their shadows were tangled together. Like a shifter's shadows."

"It was only after *that* that Rhianne's daughter came to the tree where her mother had died." Allie pressed her fingers against her eyes, as if to keep them open.

I wrapped my arm around her shoulders. "Go ahead. Sleep. I'll wake you if anyone comes."

Allie hunched in on herself. "I sound all stupid and scared, don't I?"

"It isn't stupid to be scared when the danger's real. And the moment I hear anything, I'll wake you. I promise." I could at least do that much.

"All right." Allie sighed, a sound troubled as the wind before a storm, and shifted to rest her head on my thigh. It took a while, but eventually her eyes closed, and her breath relaxed into sleep.

I kept watch, listening for noises in the dark, long past when the purple light dimmed and went out.

~~ *Chapter 6* ~~

It was smell, not sound, that warned me of Nys's approach, the aroma of some roasted root vegetable. I nudged Allie awake as purple light flickered in the dark and Nys stepped out of another tunnel that hadn't been there before. I put myself between him and Allie, gauging the distance to that tunnel. The ache had left my hip and leg. We might have a chance, if we ran.

Nys followed my gaze and raised an eyebrow, as if my thoughts of escape amused him. He touched the wall, and the tunnel closed. He wouldn't have done that if he truly believed escape impossible.

"I said I would bring food." Nys held the bowl out to us.

Allie grabbed my arm as she backed away, pulling me with her. The amusement drained from Nys's face.

"Eat it. Or must I enchant you to make you do even this small thing?"

Allie's grip tightened, but then she let go and stalked forward. Not under glamour—the anger in those steps was every bit Allie's. "Give it to me. I can eat on my own."

Nys handed her the bowl. "It is good to see one of you thinking sensibly. Humans are fragile enough when they do eat."

There was no fork. Allie shoved a pale white tuber into her mouth with her fingers and chewed, glaring at Nys all the while. I thought of stories from Before, about the dangers of eating faerie food—but surely the food wasn't the greatest danger here.

I met Nys's stony gaze. "If you knew Allie at all, you'd know you don't need magic to get her to heal."

"I know she has said as much. I know, too, how little human words can be trusted. The humans who asked to meet with us before the Uprising assured us they meant no harm."

I stayed close to Allie's side as she ate. "No one with magic can lie."

"This is so among my own true folk," Nys said. "It may or may not be true among humans, and besides, truth is a slippery thing. Given freedom to act, the healer could as easily use her magic to kill as to heal."

"I'd never do that!" Allie's cheeks flushed with anger. "There's only two times it's okay to kill with healing magic: when someone is in pain and when someone's causing it." Allie handed me the half-empty bowl, but her glare remained fixed on Nys. "Magic is for help, not harm. You of all people should know that, living in the place where magic began."

Magic had done harm enough during the War. Allie knew that as well as me. Yet she went on. "The oath came from your people, didn't it? It didn't come from mine. Until the War, we didn't have any magic to make oaths about."

"An oath. About magic." Nys's arms moved to his sides, one hand resting on his stone belt. A watchful posture, like mine when I was thinking of drawing my knife. "Tell me about this oath, Healer."

Stones *were* weapons for Nys. I set the bowl down, leaving my good hand free. Allie pressed her lips together, angry still, and she repeated the words I'd spoken for Karin when I became her student, words Allie must have once spoken for Caleb, too:

> *Blessed are the powers that grant me*
> *   magic.*
> *I promise to use their gift well.*
> *To help mend my world,*

To help mend all worlds.
And should I forget to mend,
Should I refuse to mend,
Still I will remember
To do no harm.

"If I do any harm," Allie said, "it'll be by accident or because you make me do it. But I'll never do harm on purpose, never."

"Tell me, child. Where did you learn that?" So cold, Nys's voice. It made the room feel colder, too.

"From my teacher," Allie said.

"And who would your teacher be?"

Allie glanced at me. I shook my head. There were faerie folk enough who blamed Caleb for starting the War.

"I could compel you to tell me, but in this case there is hardly the need." Nys's hand left his belt. "I know my eldest son's work well enough, for good and for ill. I hear him in every word of this oath you speak. Tell me, is Kaylen well?"

"You're Caleb and Karin's *father*?" Allie blurted. I stared at Nys, knowing my face showed how startled I was as clearly as Allie's words.

"Oh, not Karinna's." Nys sounded affronted. "I'm nowhere near that old. But I asked you a question. Answer it."

Information was a weapon, too. "Promise you won't use glamour on either of us," I said. "Only then will we tell you how Caleb is."

"I could make the healer answer," Nys said. "I cannot control her thoughts, but I think I could draw information from her."

"But Caleb wouldn't want you to." Allie's hands went to her hips. "You know he wouldn't."

"Do not attempt to shame me, child. I know my son's mistakes well enough. All the Realm knows Kaylen's mistakes, just as all have known his true name since those mistakes became known. Much harm followed, when he withdrew his glamour from a human. Has he told you that story?"

"The War followed." I knew the story better than Nys could imagine, because the human was my mother; knew, too, that no war was so simple as to be caused by any one person. "Your promise," I said. "You can compel Allie with glamour, but you cannot compel me, and as a seer I know things about Caleb she does not."

Nys turned away. Allie picked up the bowl, held it out to me. I ate what remained of the tubers. They held an overripe sweetness, near to rotting, that made me want to gag.

Only as Allie set down the bowl did Nys turn back to us. "So long as you do as I say, I'll not use glamour on either of you." He spoke slowly, as if the words came at some cost.

"So long as we do no harm," I insisted.

"And how does a human account harm? No. I have offered more than you deserve. I'll offer no more—and Elin and I *will* have words about her keeping this from me."

Allie looked at me, and this time I nodded. "Caleb was fine when we left him," she said. "He teaches humans now. Not only me." She stopped there, with no mention of Mom or the baby. Good.

Silence. I waited. I'd learned, as Karin's student, that faerie folk didn't feel the need to fill the quiet with words as so many humans did.

Something in Nys's expression thawed. "For this news, much thanks. Though Kaylen is no longer welcome in the Realm, nor within the shelters I built for our people here, knowing he survived the human Uprising means a great deal to me. My visions have been unclear on this matter, but they don't reach as far as they once did. Those visions told me Kaylen survived for a time, but not how long. What do your seer's visions say of him, Liza?"

"Caleb's coming here." I made no mention of Matthew, told Nys no more than I had to.

Allie's eyes grew large, hopeful—and then Nys's

hands snaked out to grasp my shoulders. "Why would he do such a thing?"

I drew my dead hand to my side, knowing I'd have little chance if I fought him here, with unbroken stone all around. "He comes looking for his student, and for his sister, and for—" What relation were Caleb and I? "And for me."

Nys's fingers dug through my sweater, bruising me. "Kaylen and Karinna are not friends. He would not come for her."

"Yet they've always tried to protect each other." I knew that from my visions.

The links of Nys's belt shifted, clinking restlessly against one another. "Kaylen ought not to return. He'll not live long if he does. The border protections the Lady put in place shortly after the Uprising will destroy him and any who enter the Realm with him."

"Border protections?" My voice echoed off the stone around us, unnaturally loud.

"The ruler of the Realm is tied to this land in ways the rest of us can scarcely imagine. If she truly wishes to keep someone out, she can do so. No doubt the Lady had her reasons, just as she had her reasons for seeing to it that seers can no longer leave the ways between our worlds idly open. You won't hear me suggest it was something so simple as anger at her youngest son, or anything aside from the good of the Realm, that dictated her actions."

Allie and I exchanged a look. Caleb was walking—no, running—into a deadly trap. *And any who enter the Realm with him.* Matthew, too. The cold light couldn't lessen the room's chill. "We have to stop him."

"We need do no such thing." Nys released my shoulders. I stumbled back. "Kaylen made his decisions long ago, and if he suffers the consequences of them, he is hardly alone in that." Nys reached for Allie. "Now. Show me that humans can keep their promises."

Allie bit her lip. "It doesn't have to be one thing or the other. We could go after Caleb when the healing's through."

"Through?" Nys said, as if he didn't understand. "You do not appreciate the extent of the harm your people wrought. This will never be through, not until the Realm itself crumbles away. We ease the worst of their suffering, nothing more." His fingers closed around Allie's wrist. "Since the War, I have done all I can for my people. I will continue to do so, and if there are prices to be paid, I will pay them. Come, Healer."

"Wait," I said. "The border magic. How can it be undone?" Maybe we could save Caleb and Matthew, even if we couldn't get free ourselves.

"Undone?" Nys's laughter was rough as stone

scraping stone. "It cannot be undone, save by the Lady or her heir. The one is gone and the other lacks wit enough to act. Unless you'd like to attempt to slit Karinna's throat, as I have vowed to Elin not to, in hopes that the power will fall to the weaver. I would not stop you. Karinna and I are not friends, either, for all that I've thrown my lot in with her daughter, who believed Karinna's presence might be of use to the land. Kaylen would have been a far more suitable heir—but the time for such maneuvering is past. Until very recently, I was not aware Karinna lived. Now, Liza, must I bind you to the wall again, or will you allow Allie and I to depart in peace?"

"I'll be all right," Allie said softly. "Trust me."

It was Nys I didn't trust, but angering him might lose us a chance at escape later. "There's no need to bind me. I won't try to stop you."

"You cannot stop us. Remember that." Nys touched the wall. Stone melted away, a tunnel appeared, and Nys and Allie walked into it. I focused on my breathing once more as I forced myself not to follow them, watching as the tunnel disappeared, taking Nys's light with it and leaving me in the dark.

I slept, not because sleeping was safe, but because if I didn't, I would lose my edge, like a dulled blade.

When I woke, Tolven stared silently down at me, a

glowing stone in his cupped hands. His silver eyes were wild, his breath ragged. I scrambled to my feet, forcing the sleep from my thoughts as I crouched into a defensive stance. How long had he stood there? His muscles tensed, as if preparing to attack—or struggling not to. I held my hands up, a sign that I wouldn't attack if he didn't.

Tolven's breathing steadied, and one side of his mouth quirked into what might have been a smile. "I will not hurt you." His nails were clipped short now, but his hands tugged restlessly at his sleeves. "I will only listen. The green you carry is not so troubling, once one stops trying to fight it. That is difficult, but difficult is not the same as impossible."

There was a tunnel open behind him. I rocked on my heels, as if to back away, then lunged forward, grabbed the stone from Tolven's hands, and ran toward it.

A whisper of ice brushed my face. I caught the scent of something musty and old as gray dust trickled to the floor in front of me.

I skittered to a halt. A fist-sized patch of darkness sank like mist through a hole in the ceiling. I felt Tolven's hand on my shoulder, pulling me back from it.

"*Go away!*" I commanded the dark, but it just kept sinking down, down, down. The purple light grew gray and thin as color drained from the room and the air took on the bleak chill of a rainy winter morning. I smelled the decay of leaf mold, the rot of old meat. The empty food bowl disappeared into the darkness. That darkness sank through the floor and was gone, leaving behind a pile of gray dust where the bowl had been.

"Close." Tolven released his hold and stepped around me to block the tunnel. "Too close. Do all humans move with more haste than care?"

Color seeped back into the room like dye through wool. It hadn't been lack of care that had made me seize a chance of escape. "What *was* that?" I eyed Tolven and the tunnel behind him, weighing other means of escape, thinking of how he had pulled me back from the dark.

He could as easily have pushed me into it, had he wanted to. I waited, tense, listening.

Tolven laughed uneasily. His hair was tied back from his face, twisted into a clear tail that fell down his back, making his eyes large and giving his face the openness of a deer on a path, in the heartbeats before it becomes aware of the hunter. "Surely the Realm's crumbling is of no surprise to humans? You sent the fires that caused it, did you not?" He tilted his head, as if uncertain. His gaze was clear, nothing wild in it now.

"You're—"

"Sane?" More laughter, gentle laughter that made me think him amused with himself. "I suppose I am, if anyone in the Realm can be deemed so now. It is the seeds you carry. Once I push past the fear, their voices are louder than the voice of the crumbling, and when I let myself listen to them, I regain my own mind. It is a strange thing, to be in control of my thoughts after so long." He held out his hand. "Give them to me, please."

I felt the velvet tug of glamour in his words, but it was weaker than Nys's, a small thing beside the pull of the seeds in my pocket. Could they truly heal a broken mind? The seed Karin had kept hadn't helped her.

"You are human," Tolven said, "yet my words do not touch you. Why?"

I dared not tell him the seeds were all that protected me from losing my mind in an entirely different way than he had, losing it to the force of his words.

"I could try to take them." Tolven shrugged good-naturedly. "But I am guessing you have other defenses in addition to those against glamour."

The seeds were my defenses—I didn't say that, either. Maybe there was a chance here, a chance to get Allie and myself free, not through fighting but through words. Faerie folk took words seriously. "If I shared the seeds with you, would you lead us back aboveground?"

Tolven rubbed his hands over his sleeves. I saw the faint bulge of bandages beneath them. "Above is fire fever, and what little grows there is far more mad than me. Below is shelter. Below is safety. There is nowhere else, save for the human world, which was so perilous it killed the Lady herself."

"Below isn't safe for humans." I looked from Tolven to the tunnel. It had opened for him, as it wouldn't for me. "Can you lead us out?" If we could reach the standing stone, perhaps Allie and I could get Karin out of Faerie through the Arch and stop Caleb and Matthew from trying to enter it at the same time.

"I can lead you. All the tunnels open for me. Nys saw to it, after the Uprising. None dare deny me free passage." Tolven flashed a small, secretive smile. Who was he, that his desires were considered so important? "If I free you and your friend, you will surrender the seeds?"

I chose my words carefully. "If you take Allie and me to the standing stone—the one by the ring of dead trees—I will give you *one* of the seeds. You have my word."

"Do humans keep their word?" Tolven asked me.

"Humans with magic do." Then, "I do, and would even without magic."

"So it is with me as well." Tolven bent into a respectful bow. "I will risk this thing. I must leave now, but I shall return for you and the other human as I may. Until that time you must stay here, lest you upset Nys and so fall beyond my reach. See to it that you keep your word. None will treat you well should they learn that you harmed me."

We just might get out of here after all. I offered Tolven the stone, because Nys would know someone had been here if he saw it. Tolven took it and left the room without another word. The tunnel closed behind him.

The stench of decay lingered in the air, but if any more crumbling approached, it was swallowed by the room's own dark. I kept to the far side of the room, and I did not sleep again.

I knew Allie's approach by the light she held. She shuffled down a tunnel—yet another tunnel—and into the room, a wine skin over her shoulder and another bowl of food in her hands. The tunnel closed behind her as she stumbled to my side. I caught her and helped her sit leaning against the wall, carefully steering her away from the dust. Its smell had faded, but I didn't know how long it would remain dangerous to touch. Allie's hands trembled as she set the bowl on the floor between us. Her eyes were ringed with dark shadows.

"He promised not to use glamour." I handed Allie a vegetable from the bowl. If Nys wasn't bound to keep his word, we had no power over him at all.

"He didn't use it." Allie chewed listlessly on the tuber. "I pushed a little too hard, that's all. I wanted to prove I would do as I said so that he wouldn't change his mind and take me over after all." Her voice was heavy with shadows of its own. "It was much better, with me doing things for myself. Only"—she reached for another vegetable—"I saw two more patients. One I could save, but the other slipped away faster than I could heal him. That happens sometimes. I know it does. It's not like I haven't seen people die, but Caleb was always there with me before. I was never alone." She squeezed her eyes shut.

I couldn't make that right. I put my arm around her shoulders instead.

"It's all right. Nys didn't blame me, so that was good." Allie opened her eyes. "It's so sad, the way fire fever makes everything come unraveled deep inside of them."

I shivered. "Unraveling and crumbling. They're sort of the same, aren't they?"

Allie shuddered. "Don't say that."

"Is it true?"

"I don't know," Allie said. "The squirrel—it was only its body crumbling away, not its . . . its essence. That's true for fire fever, too. The man who died . . . what you would call his shadow, it left him. It didn't unravel like his body was doing. But that's also true for all sorts of illnesses that have nothing to do with the crumbling. Don't scare me."

"I'm not saying it to scare you." I was saying it because when Allie healed, she was touching the fire fever as surely as she'd touched the crumbling squirrel. "I'm saying it so you'll be careful."

"Of course I'm careful!" Allie bit fiercely into the rest of her tuber. "But of course I'm going to do all I can, and not just because we're trapped here and I have no choice. Nys doesn't understand that. It's so strange that he's Caleb's father, isn't it? I think it's because of Caleb he decided to trust me a little, but he doesn't trust you. I don't know why."

Perhaps it was because I would still take out his eyes, given the chance. I had little talent for hiding such things. I needed to learn to hide them. "You're Caleb's student," I said. "And I'm Karin's."

"I don't see why—" Allie picked up another tuber, turned it in her hand.

"I think faerie politics are complicated, and I think Caleb and Karin used to be on different sides of them." I took a vegetable from the bowl, too, doing my best to ignore the slimy way it slid down my throat.

Allie set her tuber back in the bowl, uneaten. "I'm so worried about them. We don't know if Karin's even alive, and Caleb—he'll do anything to get to us."

"I know." I rubbed at my shoulder, but I couldn't

reach all the sore spots on my own. Lowering my voice, I said, "Matthew's with him."

"Of course he is. Don't need visions to see that." Allie wrapped her arms around herself. "I'm tired, but it doesn't seem right to sleep when so many people I care about are in so much trouble."

"If you rest, you'll be better able to help them."

"I know that. I do." Allie sipped from the wine skin. "You need sleep, too, Liza." She handed me the skin.

I drank as well. "I slept while you were gone. Go ahead."

"All right." Allie pillowed her head in my lap, and this time she fell asleep as easily as after a day's work in the fields. I brushed her hair back from skin clammy with sweat.

I watched for patches of darkness, for any scent of decay, and most of all for Tolven to keep *his* promises.

Tolven didn't return. I kept watching long after Allie's light went out, but when I saw new light in the distance at last, it was Nys, come to fetch Allie away once more.

⤙ *Chapter 7* ⤚

Allie woke at that light, and we both stood to face the stone shaper. He ignored us, kneeling instead to examine the pile of gray dust. He tapped his belt, and one of the links took on a liquid brightness. He drew the link free, and it shifted into a sharp stone shard. Nys poked the shard into the dust, removed it, and, finding it whole, pressed it back into his belt, where it became ordinary stone once more. He put his hands to the floor on either side of the dust then, and that stone, too, turned to shining liquid. Sweat trickled down Nys's face as the liquid rock flowed over the dust, covering it before hardening again.

"That should hold well enough," Nys said. "And so you see more of the damage the Uprising has wrought. Come, Healer."

Had the fires my people sent truly caused this crumbling, as surely as they'd caused the unraveling of fire fever? How could any fire hold that much power?

Allie let Nys's fingers wrap around hers. I wanted to throw up the sickly sweet vegetables I'd eaten. How many times would I watch, powerless, as he took Allie away?

"Take me with you," I said. Allie shouldn't have to do this alone—and beyond this room, there might be some chance of escape. Tolven hadn't come back. It was up to us to find our own way out.

"And why would I do that?" Nys looked coolly down at me. "You're no healer. You can draw the living to you, but you cannot call back the dead."

"But she can," Allie said. "If they haven't gone too far."

"Indeed?" Nys tightened his hold on the healer. "That is not a power summoners were known to have, before the Uprising."

Karin hadn't told me that. I fought to keep the surprise from my face. "I can help Allie. If someone's shadow tries to slip away again, I can call it back, at least for a little while. I can give her more time."

Nys went very still. "I do not know whether to welcome your help or kill you for having such unnatural power."

"I'm of more use to your people alive," I said.

Nys gave me a long, level look. "That is a near thing. See that you do not take it for granted. I will hold your hand. If you cause any trouble, you will pay for it."

I did not need to ask which hand he meant. I swallowed and held my left hand out to him. Nys's free hand wrapped around mine. His touch shivered through the stone, a reminder of how much power he had over it. My stomach churned. Nys walked swiftly into the tunnel, and Allie and I followed. Allie walked steadily, head held high. There was something in that posture—she hadn't just gotten taller this past year. She'd gotten older, nearer to the adult she would be. I hadn't noticed, living with her day to day.

We turned into another tunnel, one with more glowing purple stones embedded in its walls. Side passages branched off the main one. From one corridor I heard soft voices reciting poetry, something about swift red hawks and slow green trees, things that must have been as lost to this world's Before as cars and telephones were lost to mine. From another corridor, I caught a glimpse of warm yellow light. I glanced down that corridor, into a huge room filled with dark soil and brown leafy trees and vines. Winter colors, only the plants weren't limp like winter plants. Somewhere among them somebody sang a strange, low song, filled with the sounds of wind blowing, rain falling, plants sighing as they reached for the sun, a song that made me long for any world beyond these tunnels. Nys slowed his steps as the song stopped and a voice whimpered, "Color crumbles. Green is but a dream. Only gray remains." The singer shrieked and took up his wordless song once more. I knew him then: Tolven. He sounded lost, far too lost to help us.

"Who's that?" Allie said. "He sounds so sad. He's sick, too, isn't he?"

"It is not an illness you can mend. Healers cannot heal everything. Surely Kaylen has taught you this." Nys strode on, and Allie and I scrambled to keep up as Tolven's voice faded. Light reflected off clear gems set in the tunnel's ceiling and floor, casting rainbows through the air ahead of us.

Allie reached out, as if to catch the colors in her hand. "Mind hurts. We can't heal mind hurts."

"Just so." Nys walked through the light as if he scarcely noticed it. "Our young plant speaker is quite mad, and no wonder. He came into his magic as the fire fell from the skies. The first thing he heard was the trees' screams as they died. He hears them still, in memory and in every twisted plant he calls. Nothing grows straight or true here any longer. It is more than any speaker can endure. Thanks to Karinna, we know that for certain now."

"He wouldn't hear dying plants in my world," I said.

Even in winter, human plants merely slept, and in summer they grew strong enough to seek human blood. "You
could send him there." Karin and Allie and I weren't the
only ones who needed to escape this place.

Nys jerked me forward, and heat flared through my
hand. "Do you condemn us all so lightly? Since the Uprising, precious little grows here without help. Most of
our other plant speakers perished in the fighting. The
few who remained here to protect us fell to fire fever
soon after. Without poor Toby, we would surely per-
ish as well. Even with him our crops failed for a time,
without warning or reason. There is no telling when that
might happen again."

Toby, Nys had called him. That had to be his short-
name, making Tolven his true one after all. He had to be
mad indeed to give it to me.

Allie's steps stiffened, not with glamour, but with
anger. "It's wrong. Keeping him here."

"And what would you know of what's right or wrong
for my people? We may all fall to the fire fever and the
crumbling in the end, but I'll delay that day as long as I
can. We all bear scars from this War, some more openly
than others. If Toby pays a higher price than most, there
is no helping that."

An open archway stood at the end of the corridor. A
woman in a green tunic and pants was stationed there,

a long knife at her belt. She scowled when she saw us. "Another human?"

"I take full responsibility for her," Nys said. "We have need of healers, and of other magics as well. Unless your fear is greater than your will to help our people." The contempt in his words would have been a match for the Lady herself.

"I am not afraid, I assure you," the woman said, but her hand moved toward her knife, belying her words. Nys's gaze swept into the room. It was lit by purple lights, warmed by orange ones, and held a sickly sweet sickbed scent that reminded me of the overripe vegetables I'd eaten. The ill lay on the floor, furs beneath them and down blankets covering them. A few other fey folk tended to them. Patients and visitors alike were quiet, far quieter than most sick humans would have been.

Nys stopped beside a man whose clear hair lay around his face like a cloud. The stone shaper released Allie's hand but held tight to mine. "You will start here today, Healer."

Allie knelt beside the man. His eyes were closed, but his body held none of the restfulness of sleep. I started toward her side. Nys pulled me back. "You will not interfere. You will only watch their shadows, and call if calling is needed."

I hadn't been trying to interfere, only to help. I

watched the man's shadow from where I stood. It was solid and dark within him, trembling as the man was not.

Allie pulled the blanket back, her attention already more on her patient than on Nys or me. Deep red bruises mottled the man's too-tight skin, and the bones beneath pressed against it, as if seeking to break free. Allie ran her hands over his body with a series of light touches, none lasting too long. The man's dull silver eyes opened to regard her without curiosity.

Allie bit her lip and put her hands to his chest. I kept my own gaze on his shadow, watching for any sign of fading or flickering. Light bloomed gently beneath Allie's hands, hundreds of thin silver threads that formed a shimmering web as they burrowed into the man's skin. For a moment it seemed I saw through flesh to where those threads wove their way into blood and bone, making it whole, and then the light was gone. Allie smiled wearily. "You need rest now," she said. More light flashed over his body, and his shadow stopped trembling as he shut his eyes. Allie sighed and drew her hands away. The man's red bruises were gone.

"Will he live?" Nys asked, his voice cold.

"I hope so." Allie gasped for breath between words, as if she'd been running. "It's so much more work to heal your people than mine, because they're so much stronger—and fire fever is slippery. Sometimes I'm sure

I've gotten it all, but other times, like this one, it's hard to tell." Allie's shoulders slumped as her breath steadied. "I'm sorry."

"It's not your fault," I said. Allie and I hadn't commanded the fire that fell from the skies, any more than we'd ordered the trees to attack my people. Yet the harm those things had left behind was ours to live with, just the same.

"All humans share the blame for what happened here." Nys moved to a woman's side. "This one next, Healer." The woman's eyes were closed, but air rasped in and out of her lungs as if through dry leaves. I saw a deer's shadow tangled with her human one.

Allie looked up at us, and there was something in her eyes. *Too far,* I thought. She was afraid of pushing too far. Allie pressed her lips together and knelt by the woman's side.

"She needs rest," I said. "Before she does any more."

Allie shook her head, a warning. Nys's fingers tightened around mine. My fingers tightened around *his,* and heat pulsed through them. I stumbled, and the heat went away, but my fingers remained obediently in place, as if I were a child holding an adult hand. I wanted to throw up. It took all my will not to fight that hold.

"Go on, Healer," Nys said. "I will tell you when you may stop."

Allie lifted the blanket, while other faerie folk in the room watched us in silence. I swallowed the sour taste in my mouth. Even if I could escape Nys's hold, there were too many others. We weren't leaving until Nys said we were.

Allie ran her hands over the woman's body, stopped, and glanced at me. "Shifter?" she asked, and I nodded. Allie's hands moved to the woman's breastbone. Light bloomed again, brighter and more focused, a river of light that flowed into her.

"Does it please you, Liza, to watch our people die?" Nys's gaze remained on Allie and the woman she healed. "To know that we have been dying ever since your petty Uprising?"

"No. It doesn't please me." Perhaps it should have, trapped as I was by those people, but it made me feel as ill as the way my fingers remained wrapped around Nys's.

"We once thought those few of our people who survived the initial burning were fortunate. We were wrong. The fires burn within as well as without. Only the worst come to this sickroom, but none is untouched by this illness that continues to cling to air and soil and stone."

I watched as Allie drew away. My people had died, too, in the War. They had not died slowly.

"That one was easier," Allie said. "The fever wasn't

everywhere, just in one place. When she's strong enough to shift, I'll need to see her again to be sure, but I think she'll be okay." As Allie stood, Nys grasped her hand again. "I really do need rest now," the healer said, her voice small.

"And you shall have it." Nys turned and swept from the room, pulling us after him. Allie stumbled as she hurried to keep up. We turned down the main hall and moved steadily through it, past all the side passages. They were no longer lit, and I didn't hear Tolven's voice as Nys led us back to our room.

"You have done good work this day, Healer. For that, much thanks." Nys released Allie's hand but held mine a moment more. "You please me less, Liza. You will not accompany us again." I felt my stone fingers unwrap from around his, one by one. Nys left us, taking the light. I ran after him, but of course I wasn't fast enough. The stone closed behind him, leaving us in the dark.

"He has to take you next time!" Allie cried. "We have to find a way out!" Her shadow hand searched for mine, and her fingers gripped the stone, though I couldn't feel it. "We can't let Caleb and Matthew come here. We *can't*."

"I know that!" I jerked away with more force than intended. "Don't you think I know?" I was failing them all: Matthew, Caleb, Karin, Allie. Allie fumbled for me again, but I stepped out of her reach. My stone hand felt heavy and dead by my side. None of us was going to make it out of here, not now, not ever.

"Liza?" Allie's voice was small. "Don't be angry, please. Don't leave me alone here."

I drew a deep breath, focusing on the feel of air moving into my chest. Breathe in. Breathe out. I could not afford to lose control. "Sorry, Allie." With my good hand, I reached for her.

Stone whispered over stone, and an arm snaked around my neck.

"Seeds," Tolven rasped.

～ *Chapter 8* ～

"*G*o *away!*" I whispered the command as his grip tightened. *"Tolven, go away!"*

Abruptly he released me. "You promised seeds," he pouted. "The green is real. Nothing else is real, but the green *is*. And you promised."

I gasped for air, my hand going to my throat. "I promised you one seed, and I promised it later. After you lead us away from here. Remember?"

"Remembering's hard," Tolven whined. "Too many other voices. Too many—" His own voice rose, cracked. "I can listen. Listen to the green. I did it before. I will do it now." For several heartbeats I heard only his ragged breathing. Then, "I am sorry. Did I harm you?"

"We're fine," I said, knowing he was himself again.

"And I will give you a seed, just as soon as you show us the way out."

Allie edged close to me and took my hand. I squeezed it, willing her to feel my apology. She squeezed back, and I hoped she forgave me.

"I got lost again," Tolven said softly. "I knew I had to find the seeds, but I could not recall why, through the wilting and the crumbling all around. I am weary of being lost—that is not your concern. We have made a bargain, and I will keep it. Come, this way."

My throat hurt. I wanted to say it was my concern, though I had little enough reason to trust Tolven beyond the promises we'd exchanged. His shadow moved silently across the room, and I followed, leading Allie behind me. Maybe the seed would be enough to save him. But it hadn't been enough for Karin.

Light flooded the room as a tunnel opened before us. "Even mad, I knew I could not be seen," Tolven said matter-of-factly. There were new tears along his sleeves, stained with dried blood. He took the purple stone that lay in the tunnel in his hand. "I hid the light in one passage, then came for you through another."

By the light, I saw the wine skin Nys had given us lying on the floor. I ran back to sling it over my shoulder, and then Allie and I followed Tolven into the tunnel. We swiftly reached a stone wall, but the stone parted at Tolven's approach, revealing a longer passage with rougher walls. As we entered that tunnel, I heard the groan of shifting rock. I looked back to see the stone closing in behind us, leaving us only a few free paces ahead and behind. *A trap,* I thought, but Tolven kept walking, and the stone kept opening ahead of him, as quickly as it closed behind. I pushed Allie in front of me; if one of us got caught by the swift-flowing stone, I didn't want it to be her. Allie gave me a long look and dropped back to my side, though there was barely room for the two of us to walk abreast. Our steps echoed against the tunnel floor.

"Not so loud." Tolven scowled as he glanced back at us. "Do you wish to be found?"

I knew how to walk more quietly, but not without slowing down. With the stone flowing behind us, I chose speed over stealth. We climbed uphill, gently at first, then more steeply, until I heard my and Allie's breaths as well as our steps.

Without warning, Tolven stopped, one hand halfway to the stone ahead of us. "The Summoner's Grove—what remains of the Grove—is just beyond this spot. You will give me the seed so I can see that humans keep their word, and then I will step forward and the stone will open to that place. When it does, you will be free to leave." He extended his hand to me.

I reached into my pocket and took out a seed. The life in all the seeds flared stronger, as if they were reluctant to be parted from one another. I pressed the seed into Tolven's palm. His fingers closed around it, and I felt . . . peace, flowing like a contented sigh from the green he held. Or maybe it came from Tolven himself, who set his glowing stone aside to cradle the seed in both hands like a precious child. "Yes. It is well done."

Cold tickled the back of my neck. I turned to see the way behind us filling with a darkness the light could not touch. Dust trickled to the floor a couple arms' lengths away, no more. The purple light gave way to gray.

"Tolven," I said.

Tolven looked up from the seed, as if waking from a dream, to focus on the gray all around us. He moved swiftly forward. Stone flowed aside, letting in hot yellow sun. Allie and I stepped past him into a world of blue sky, glittering ash, black tree snags. My eyes ached at the sudden brightness. In the distance, I saw a circle of stumps, bench and standing stone within them.

"You should go," Tolven said as the darkness drew closer behind him.

I hesitated, then held out my hand. "Come with us," I said, hoping I wasn't making a mistake. For the first time, I wondered what it had been like for Karin and Caleb, offering help to an unknown town, not certain how far its humans could be trusted. "The trees aren't dying in our world."

"A worthy offer." Tolven took the purple stone in one hand. The other closed around the seed. "And a tempting one." He looked at me with his open gaze. "Yet while my thoughts remain my own, I think I might do my people some good below. Do humans accept bonds of friendship with my people?"

"Some of us do." A breath of ice blew from the tunnel. The dark was only a foot or so from Tolven. "I do."

"Me too," Allie said. Her town had accepted faerie folk and their magic long before mine.

"In that case, should there come a time when I can be of no further use to my world, I will seek you in yours. Until then, travel well." Tolven bowed, more deeply than before, and turned to the tunnel wall. A new passage opened off of it, and he disappeared into it.

"He shouldn't go back!" Allie cried as the stone closed behind him. "They don't deserve him, not after they held him here when they *knew* they could set him free."

They didn't deserve him, but I was beginning to think that wasn't the point. "Did the people you healed deserve it?"

"That's different! They were sick, and no one can help that!"

Maybe none of us were worthy enough to deserve the good things that happened to us. I inhaled hot wind and open sky like a gift. Together Allie and I left the tunnels behind, walking swiftly through a world of color and light.

~ *Chapter 9* ~

Ash burned the soles of my bare feet as we walked. Sun shone on the snags of dead trees, and I kept blinking the dryness from my eyes.

"Do you think Toby will be okay?" Hot wind blew strands of Allie's red hair into her face.

I glanced back. How long did we have before Nys found us gone? "I don't know." As we neared the more ordered circle of snags surrounding the standing stone, I saw the one stump among them that wasn't dead. Wider around than my arms could reach, that tree stretched shadow branches like gnarled fingers toward the sky. Karin crouched before it. Allie tightened her grip as I let out a breath. Karin was alive. It was almost more than I'd hoped for. Elin hovered protectively beside her. Karin made soft crooning sounds as she rocked back and forth. She lived, but her mind was still not her own.

"I hear you well enough, Liza." Elin did not turn from her mother. Beside them, a bowl held a few pale tubers. "Allie, too. There is no sense trying to sneak up on me. My people do not need rest so often as yours do, with every fleeting cycle of the sun."

I hadn't been trying to sneak up on her. It was Elin who'd snuck into my house, stealing me away. "Let us take Karin out of here, Elin. You must know she can't stay in Faerie."

Elin laughed, a sound jagged as broken glass. "You think it an easy thing, to lead my mother away? You are welcome to do so, then." She stepped aside. Beneath her green cloak, a short knife and several small pouches hung from her belted brown dress.

I released Allie to approach Karin, fearing some trap. Karin gave a small cry and cupped her hands around something. A thin brown stem, sprouting from the stump. A tiny round leaf unfurled from it. The leaf nuzzled her palm, wilted, and fell to the ashes at her feet. The plant speaker let out a high, animal wail.

"Karin." I reached for her.

She whirled around, her fist striking my side so hard and fast it knocked the breath from me. I fell to the ground, one ankle twisting with a sickening lurch. Karin squinted, as if puzzled she could not see me, then turned back to the tree and began crooning once more.

"Do you think me a fool?" Elin's voice came through a haze of pain as Allie pressed hands to my foot. "Of course I would take her out of here if I could. As one of the first line, I can cross between our worlds as easily as any seer. But lost though my mother's mind may be, gone though her sight may be, her warrior's skills have not abandoned her. I have been no more able to get near her than you."

"Your ankle's not broken," Allie said. "Just sprained. Here." A flash of cold silver light took the pain away. Allie sat back, breathing hard. "That was . . . harder than I expected. I really did push hard, down below. I'd tell you not to walk on it, but we don't have a choice, do we?"

I stood, watching as Karin called another brown shoot. *"Karinna!"* I called with my magic. *"Come here!"*

Karin gave no sign she heard. She just kept singing wordlessly to the new stem, until it, too, wilted away. Karin was the one person who had always been there whenever I'd called.

"She's lost her name, hasn't she?" Elin's voice was flat. "It's worse for her than for Toby. I should have expected that. She's the land's own heir now. She doesn't just hear the plants. She hears *everything.*"

"Lost names can be found," I said. Karin's shadow

remained solid within her. Something of her was yet there, if only we could reach it. I saw the shadow of the seed in her pocket as well. Was it because she heard more than Tolven did that the seed couldn't help her?

Allie moved to Elin's side and brushed fingers along storm-dark bruises at her wrist. "Karin hurt you, too." Light flowed from Allie's fingers.

Elin jerked away. "It is not broken, and it aches only lightly. Do not waste your power on me. Others need it. Nys isn't wrong about that." Elin laughed again. "I told him you would escape, one way or another, when he refused to tell me where he'd hidden you. He does not have my experience underestimating you, Liza." The laughter died. "I made my bargain with him poorly. I made him vow not to harm my mother but did not think to protect her student as well—and you, Allie, were entirely unexpected. You must know that. I was willing enough to sacrifice you both to bring my mother home, but not to turn you over to Nys." Elin's cloak rippled, though there was no wind. "As it is, my mother's presence has done little to set anything right."

Karin kept calling stems to grow and die, grow and die, while somewhere outside Matthew and Caleb moved ever closer to the Arch. I stepped toward Karin, and she stiffened. Maybe, if I kept trying, I could reach her at last.

And maybe Matthew and Caleb would die while I did. As far as I could tell, Karin had more time than they did. "You'll continue keeping watch over her?" I asked Elin.

The weaver turned to me, her silver eyes sharp. "You intend to depart the Realm without my leave? With my grandmother gone and my mother unable to speak for herself, it is me you must answer to. I'll not have you forget that, Liza."

None of this would have happened if not for Elin. "Caleb heads this way, Matthew with him." I fought to keep the anger from my voice. "Toward the Arch. As the Lady's heir, perhaps you know what that means?"

"Kaylen is coming here?" Elin's hands twisted in the fabric of her cloak. Did she blame him, as so many did, for starting the War? "Yes, of course he is." She looked to her mother. "Is there no end to the sacrifices you will both make for humans?"

"Is it true?" Allie asked. "Will coming here really kill him?"

"Oh yes." Elin turned abruptly from her mother and strode to the standing stone. Allie and I looked at each other.

"Well, come on, then," Elin said. "Someone needs to see to it that you do not die, as humans tend to do."

We stared at her, wary of some new trap. Elin sighed.

"When my people make a mistake, we try to set things right. It may be different among humans, but even so, I will accompany you on this journey. As far as I can tell, even with her mind gone, Karinna the Fierce remains quite capable of protecting herself and no more requires my presence than she ever did. A few short days without food or drink will not hurt her, any more than a few days without sleep will hurt me."

I doubted Ethan, who'd lost his town to her, would think Elin had set anything right, but I couldn't stop her from leaving. I glanced back. Karin wept as she called another stem to grow, and another. What use was I as her student if I could not help her? I joined Elin at the standing stone. As far as I could tell, Karin would be in no greater danger if I left than if I stayed, and that wasn't true for Matthew and Caleb. Allie put one hand to my arm and reached for Elin with the other. Elin ignored her to put her own hands to the stone. "I can find my own way to the Arch, without any seer's visions to delay me." The stone turned liquid at her touch. She stepped into it and was gone.

Yellow sunlight reflected off the bright rock. *The Arch. Show me the Arch.* The light grew brighter, filling my sight, and I saw—

Karin, on her knees in the ashes of Faerie, tunic stained with blood, silver eyes dull as tarnished steel.

"This madness is welcome indeed," she whispered as she fell forward. Only then Caleb was behind her, pulling her to her feet. She fought him, hissing like some wild creature as she bent his wrist at an unnatural angle, but his fingers grabbed her wrist in turn, and in a flash of silver light she fell limp to the ground. "I'm sorry, Eldest Sister, but neither of us gets to escape all we've done so easily. You will survive this War, as will I." Caleb hefted her over his shoulders, walked toward a burning lake, and disappeared within it—

Too far. This was too far in the past. "Show me the present," I whispered, as I'd practiced with Karin so many times. The scene shifted slowly, as if the present were something my visions were reluctant to reveal, until I saw—

Matthew and Caleb running side by side, on four legs and two, running along broken black stone roads, through forests whose green was giving way to red, yellow, gold—and gray, patches of crumbling gray dust, made more dead by the bright colors around them. The wind was wild, and lightning flashed beneath a storm-tossed sky. Branches grabbed at them by day, tree shadows by night. They kept running, toward a crossroads that looked down on a mirrored silver Arch, its top hundreds of feet high, its legs hundreds of feet apart—

I stepped forward, Allie's hand on my arm. Stone and darkness closed in around me, squeezing the air from my chest. I fought for breath as my heart slowed, stopped for a beat—

—and then I staggered free, into a cold, spitting rain. Elin waited beneath one leg of the silver Arch, which was bright in spite of the thick yellow-gray clouds above. I glanced at that mirror, but no visions sought to draw me into its surface. I'd never been able to look at the Arch without visions before.

"I'd forgotten how big it was." Allie's eyes traveled up the mirror's curve. It stood on a white stone platform that had been soaked by the rain. Autumn was further along here than at home, but the yellow and orange leaves of the trees beyond the platform were broken by patches of gray, just like in my vision. Beyond the trees to the west, bluffs rose toward the sky. To the east, the broad River—which maps called the Mississippi—lapped at the platform and stretched to the far horizon.

"Are humans always so slow?" Elin asked us.

Neither Allie nor I bothered answering that. Allie looked from the Arch to me. "Do we wait here?"

I shook my head. I didn't want to risk letting Caleb and Matthew get this close. "They'll come to the crossroads." I'd seen that in my vision, though I didn't recognize all the paths they took to get there. "We'll wait there. Just to be safe." I looked to the River. Its muddy water held a dank, mildewy scent I didn't like at all.

Allie followed my gaze to the water. "Oh. Right." Her voice was small. The River would be a problem.

"You feel it, too," Elin said. It wasn't a question. "It is worse than when I last came to your world. I can almost see the unraveling threads that flow between its banks, this world's own threads, crumbling to dust."

Her words sent ice down my spine. I'd felt death enough flowing south, when I last was here. "What has the crumbling to do with the River?"

"It is your river. You would know better than me. To me it feels like a seam whose threads are giving way to the gray to which we all must soon return. My own world has been giving way to that same gray since the Uprising. If something is not done, it will fall before yours. Do you wonder, then, that I sought my mother's help to mend this?"

Raindrops trickled down my neck and beneath my sweater. Allie looked uphill along the short path to the crossroads, which we both knew from our last journey together. She reached for my good hand. "You won't let go?"

"I—" I couldn't say I hadn't let go so far. I'd let Nys take her, more than once. "Not if I can help it."

Allie laced her fingers through mine. Rain spattered her nightgown and cloak. "I won't let you go, either," she said.

Together we crossed the stone platform. Elin followed at Allie's other side.

"Stay away from the water," I told her. "No matter what it says to you."

"Do you think me a fool, who would go willingly to my death?" Elin asked. Rain beaded off her cloak, leaving it dry.

"*Liza.*" The River whispered my name as my bare feet touched the muddy forest floor. "*You return at last, as all things must. Come here. Seek sleep. Come.*"

That call pulled on some thread deep inside me, urging me toward the water. I pressed my toes into the mud, resisting as I had once before. The seeds in my pocket helped, their green tugging on that same thread, reminding me I wasn't ready to sleep, not yet. Allie's steps didn't seek the River, either, not like last time. Perhaps her seed protected her after all, from this at least.

The wind blew on. The rain fell harder as we walked through the mud, soaking my sweater and leather pants. We had no rain gear, no means of making a fire. If the rain continued for long, we'd be in a fair amount of trouble.

The trees scarcely seemed to notice either us or the rain. They bent toward the River, as if anything else were of little concern. A clump of damp gray dust fell like late-winter snow from a branch. There was an empty patch in the forest beyond it, nothing but wet gray soil. We walked swiftly around it.

"*Too long have you fought death's current,*" the River whispered to me. "*You cannot save yourself. You cannot save those you care for. Seek rest, Liza. Seek darkness. Seek peace.*"

"I can save them." I ignored the icy raindrops that hit my face, focusing on fighting the River's call, on holding Allie's hand, on walking around another patch of gray. "I will save them."

The clouds darkened. We came to a broken path among the trees—asphalt, those born Before called the black stone—and the River's voice faded as we followed it uphill, making our way between yellow-leafed ginkgoes and poplars.

At the top of the hill, the path met another road, forming a huge crossroads filled with slabs of cracked black stone. "Well done," I told Allie as we reached the crossroads' center.

She fell to her knees and threw up.

I crouched by her side and handed her the wine skin. Allie swirled the liquid in her mouth, spit it up, and drank some more. Rain dripped from her hair and mine.

"Sorry. It's just . . . the things the River said."

"Like last time?" The River's voice hadn't made her throw up last time.

Allie shook her head. "I don't want to say. Not yet."

"Indeed." Elin's face was pale, and I wondered what the River had told her. "The light dims," she said. "If we are to build shelter for the night, we must do it soon."

To the west, thunder rumbled. We had little means of shelter. "We'll gather dead wood," I said. "Search for dead grasses to lash it together." I scanned the forest around us. The crossroads was wide enough that no tree shadows should be able to reach us if we stayed near its center.

"A poor plan," Elin said. "Allow me to suggest a better one." She spread her cloak on the stones. It was still dry, as was her dress. "I am but a weaver, yet my power may be of some use here." She moved her hands over the cloak. The fabric shimmered and flowed, turning as liquid beneath Elin's touch as stone had beneath Nys's. When the light faded, Elin's cloak had grown thin as old paper with none of the brittleness, a square of cloth fifteen feet or more across.

I reached out to touch it. It felt like well-woven wool, but the rain continued to roll off as if it were nylon from Before. I looked up at Elin, not hiding my admiration.

A ghost of a smile played across her lips. "I trust you can find wood enough to fashion this into our shelter?"

"I can," I said, and headed into the forest to do so. Allie and I found some long straight branches, and Elin used them and more weaving to shape her cloak into a tent, with two rough walls to block the wind and a roof just high enough for us to sit beneath.

We huddled under it, Allie and me in our sodden clothes, Elin in her dry ones. The rain was quite heavy by then, and Allie had begun to shiver. Elin took two stones from her belt pouches and tapped them together. The larger began to glow with warm orange light. Allie and I took turns holding it, warming our wet skin and doing what we could to dry our clothes. We'd chosen as flat a spot as we could find, but rain trickled in along cracks in the rock beneath us.

"I cannot help with food," Elin said. "The forest will have to provide that once the storm passes. I'll not take food from my people for you. We struggle enough as it is. Toby—" She turned abruptly away to stare at the curtain of rain that fell from the edge of our shelter. It was full dark, and the flashes of lightning made the rain seem the edge of the world. I wondered who Tolven was to Elin, and how she would react if she knew he'd rescued us. I wondered if her people had truly gone as hungry as mine had since the War.

Allie's shivering eased. She yawned as she cupped Elin's stone in her hands. "Think you can take first watch, Liza? I'm kind of tired. I've healed so much. I know I need rest."

Elin turned back to us. "I can watch, if you trust me to do so."

I didn't trust her, but if she'd wanted to kill us, she could have left us to the weather and stayed safe and dry in her cloak. "All right," I said. I didn't know how long we'd have to wait for Matthew and Caleb, and I had to sleep sometime.

Allie and I huddled together beneath Allie's cloak, which was only damp now. I was more tired than I thought. In spite of the cold and the wet and the knowledge that the land around us could crumble without warning any time, I slept.

When I woke, the wind had died and Elin sat watching the rain's steady fall. Allie tossed restlessly in her sleep, as if at some bad dream. She'd rolled away from me. As I reached out to wake her, my good hand brushed her neck.

It burned with fever, hot as faerie wind.

⌇ *Chapter 10* ⌇

Allie blinked awake. "I don't feel so good," she whispered.

I wrapped the cloak around her as she sat up, fumbling to close it one-handed. She drained the last of the wine skin, and I held it to the dripping edge of Elin's cloak to refill it with water. I drank, then handed the skin to Elin, who silently drank as well.

Allie shivered. "Liza, how long do you think it will take for Caleb to come?"

"I don't know." I offered her the orange stone as I crawled back to her side.

Her face went pale. She lunged for the edge of the overhang and threw up on the stones beyond it, into the rain.

I gave her the skin. Allie wiped her mouth on her

cloak and took a few small sips of water, then pushed it away. My own stomach did a little flip. This was more than some reaction to the River's voice. *It's the rain and the cold,* I told myself. *Or the food in Faerie.* Lots of things could make Allie sick.

The rain was letting up. Elin drew a dried root from another belt pouch and handed it to Allie. "Chew this. It will help calm the stormy stomach that fire fever brings."

Ice trickled down my spine. "You don't know that's what she has."

Elin's expression was unreadable. "The healer knows it."

Allie bit off a piece of the root. "Sorry, Liza. The River said—but if Caleb arrives in time, it won't matter. Even a river can be wrong, can't it? I can't heal myself, but Caleb understands fire fever better than I do anyway."

"What did the River say?" The River had said many things to us last time, not all of them true.

"It knew before I did." Allie wouldn't look at me. She chewed with slow deliberateness. "It said it didn't need to call me, because it would have me soon enough. It said . . . I didn't mean to push too far! You know I didn't!"

"Fire fever is not like other illnesses." Elin's voice was

surprisingly gentle. "It is more subtle, almost as if it has a will of its own, one that is forever seeking a new way in. Our healers had much knowledge and many long seasons behind them, yet they all fell to it in the end. Nys told you nothing of this? No, of course not—and that I'd expect him to give you the same respect as our own healers shows that I grow soft indeed. My mother would be pleased." Elin's bitter laughter died on her lips. "Nys does not speak for our people, however dearly he might wish it. So long as my mother remains absent, that responsibility falls to me. Know then, Allie, that I will not forget the sacrifice you have made for our people. I will see that they do not forget it, either. It shall be remembered in our stories, for as long as we draw breath."

I didn't want it to be remembered. I wanted it not to be happening. My dead hand felt heavy in my lap. I could not fight fire fever, any more than I could fight the crumbling, and I could not use my magic to send it away.

"Thank you, Elin." Allie's voice was soft as the patter of rain against stone. "I know how much stories mean to your people. Caleb and Karin taught me that."

Elin shut her eyes, as if the words pained her. "She has truly been with you. All this time."

Karin had been with me when my own mother had failed me. I would not regret that. If she were here now, perhaps all would be well. I stared out into the night as the rain slowed. Karin's magic would be no more use against fire fever than mine.

"Liza?" Allie moved closer to me, as if I were the one who needed comforting. "I could tell you the rest of the story, if you want." It took a moment to remember which story she meant. Not the ones Elin had promised to remember her in. The one about the summoner Rhianne, whose shadow became tangled into a tree when she died.

"Which of us are you trying to distract now?" I asked Allie.

Allie laughed, but the laughter turned to coughing. I held her until the coughing eased, then offered her the water skin. She drank more deeply. "Karin says one of the jobs of stories is to take us away from where we are. It's not their only job, but it's an important one."

"My mom thinks so, too," I said.

Elin's shoulders stiffened. "What story is it you speak of?"

"The one about the First Tree," Allie told her. "Do you know it?"

The last drops of rain dripped from our shelter. Elin caught one in her hand. "I do indeed. You are not the only person my mother has told stories to."

I wouldn't feel badly for Elin now. I wouldn't forget that if not for Elin, we would not be here.

"We were at"—Allie began coughing again—"the part where Rhianne's daughter came."

"Naturally." Elin's voice held a wry edge. "If I tell this story, will you save your strength and stop trying to speak?"

Allie raised her head. "I have strength enough for a story."

Elin watched as the rain beaded on her hands. "I would tell it, just the same."

Allie reached for the water skin, shook her head, and left it beside her. "All right." She leaned against me.

Come on, Caleb, I thought. My visions had given no sense of how long his journey would take. I could take Allie and look for him, but if I took the wrong path and missed him she'd have no chance at all. I did the only thing I could: kept watch over us all while Elin told the story.

"After Rhianne's shadow found its way back to the tree where her body had perished, Rhianne's daughter—Mirinda—found her way to that same tree. Rhianne did not know her daughter at first, because Mirinda had been new-born when her mother went away." Elin rubbed at her sleeves as she spoke, as if for comfort.

"Mirinda knew her mother, though, whatever form she took." Threads broke free of the fabric to wrap around Elin's fingers. "That was because Mirinda had inherited her father's magic and was as powerful a speaker as he. Mirinda called her mother with her magic, and Rhianne—the tree that was Rhianne—heard. Rhianne knew her daughter as well then, and she felt new grief at seeing her there. The grief of a tree is a strange thing indeed."

I reached for one of the seeds in my pocket, took it in my hand. I'd so quickly grown used to their pull on me. *These seeds know you,* Karin had said. What did it mean, to be known by a seed or a tree?

"The tree answered Mirinda's call," Elin said. "It answered her grief. It stretched its branches down to offer Mirinda a single leaf, perfectly round, as quia leaves were not before summoner and tree were joined. Mirinda accepted that gift, which contained a small piece of the tree's shadow, and of her mother's shadow, and—through magic that even today we do not fully understand—some piece of Mirinda's shadow as well. Mirinda coated the leaf in silver and wore it always, the only way she had of holding her mother close." Elin scowled and let her sleeves go. They were riddled with tiny knots.

Allie hunkered down in her cloak. I dropped the

seed back into my pocket with the others and wrapped my arm around her, offering what warmth I could. The clouds were clearing, and a bitter cold was settling more deeply into the air.

"It was many years before Mirinda realized that, while she wore the leaf, time stopped its forward march. She took no joy in this, though, for by that time she had life and loves of her own, and one by one she watched them grow old and die without her." Elin tugged at a knot. It dissolved at her touch. "Mirinda returned to the tree that was also her mother, and she pleaded with Rhianne to offer this gift of long life to all her people." Elin kept melting the knots she'd made, one by one. "Mirinda said if her mother would not do this thing, she would remove the leaf she wore, and so follow those she'd already lost into death. Then Mirinda waited, not eating, growing thin, for she was stubborn indeed."

Allie laughed, her breath rasping. "Just like Caleb. And Karin. Who are—" Allie started coughing again, and her face flushed with the effort.

My chest ached. I would plead, too, if I knew who or what to plead with.

"I thought you had agreed to let me tell this story," Elin said sharply. "Karinna and Kaylen are descended from Rhianne and Mirinda, yes, as am I, as are many others who perished in the Uprising and whose names

I'll forever hold dear. All of that came later. In the time of the story, Mirinda waited, while the tree stretched its roots deeper and deeper, looking for the thing that would make Mirinda content. No one today knows all the places those roots went. We know only that at last the tree bore its first seeds—its only seeds, until the eve of the Uprising. Rhianne bid Mirinda to tell all those she cared about to eat those seeds. And so they did, save for those they planted, and thus my people received the precious gifts of protection that put us above other creatures, whether they walk on four legs or two."

Including humans, I thought, and shivered at how casually Elin dismissed us.

"Those gifts," Elin went on, as if she'd said nothing troubling, "included not only long life, but all the powers my people have in common, above and beyond their different magics—gifts such as night vision, and distance hearing, and silent walking, and all the ways in which we are both harder to hurt and harder to heal. Gifts that meant it was never again a simple matter for weather or sickness or attacks by lesser creatures to destroy us."

"Glamour, too?" I pried a loose rock free of the asphalt and tapped it against my stone hand. The rock crumbled. Road stone from Before was weaker than it looked.

"Of course glamour, too," Elin said, as if it were a small thing. Karin must have left glamour out when she'd first told Allie the story, because until recently, Allie had no more idea what glamour was than I had. Maybe Karin had thought her and Caleb's own vows not to use glamour were enough to protect us and that we would never come upon other faerie folk who'd survived the War.

"Glamour's not—it's not—" Allie struggled for breath. I stroked her hair and made shushing sounds, but she ignored me. "It's not—right. No one should use—that kind of—power." She began coughing hard, coughing and spitting up splatters of phlegm.

"You, whose people sent fire raining down from the skies, would lecture me about right and wrong?" Elin's voice held no gentleness now.

I rubbed Allie's back. "Allie and I didn't send the fires. You know that." Somewhere in the night, an owl hooted. I tensed, but there was nothing we could do about owls except hope they didn't notice us. Owls were silent as faerie folk, and since the War, they held poison in their claws.

"The fires were every human's fault." Elin sounded weary, as if repeating an old lesson. "Would you like the rest of this story or not?"

"The fires"—Allie coughed—"were wrong, too—"

"Shhhh." I drew Allie close as I picked up another stone. Flint, stronger than asphalt. I could make a weapon of it, given time, or use it to start a fire.

"We are near enough to the story's end," Elin said. "In time Mirinda passed from the Realm, but her descendants, through all the ages of stone and fire, bronze and iron, inherited their mother's gifts, though only those of the first line were granted leaves from what we now call the First Tree. As I, too, would have been had the tree not fallen to the fires."

Mom wore Caleb's leaf from that tree. Karin had a leaf from it, too, which she'd used to create the Wall around her town. "The First Tree stood that long?" Did Faerie's trees, like its people, live so much longer than those in my world?

Elin smoothed the last snags from her sleeves. "It continues to stand, if one can trust Toby's tangled words."

I remembered the tree shadow in Faerie, branches reaching like fingers toward the sky. "Toby's right."

"So Rhianne suffers with her people still." Elin sighed. Near the horizon, a waning quarter moon struggled to poke through the clouds.

The owl hooted again. Allie leaned her head on my shoulder. I dropped my flint to brush the sweaty hair from her face. Her breathing was uneven, her eyes too bright in the faint moonlight. I could call her back if I had to. That wouldn't heal her, but it might buy us some time.

Elin lifted her head. "Someone watches us. You know this?"

I hadn't known, though some part of me had been listening. I always listened, but I would never hear as well as faerie folk did. Rhianne had seen to that. What made Elin's people so much more worthy of protection than my own?

"Of course you don't know." Elin spoke as if it were my fault no tree had ever offered my people such gifts. "I will go out, then, and see to what you cannot." Elin slipped from beneath the shelter, crossing the black stone to the edge of the forest.

I crawled gently from Allie's side to stand just outside, straining to hear what Elin heard, to see what she saw—to be something other than helpless and human. A shadow flickered at the edge of my sight.

I had an instant to throw myself to the ground before the owl's talons pierced my back.

⌒ *Chapter 11* ⌒

There was fire in those talons, fire that burned deep as they dug into my shoulders, seeking muscle and bone. "Go—" My voice froze, just as my body did as I tried to beat the creature off. Emptiness swept through me, fire turning to ice as the owl's paralyzing poison took hold. Wings flapped at the corners of my sight.

Footsteps scrabbled over stone. Allie stood before me, legs trembling, face glistening with sweat. *Run, Allie.* I couldn't speak the words—any words—aloud.

She didn't run. She reached for the owl on my back. There was a flash of silver light, brighter than any glowing stone, and the wings ceased their flapping.

Allie toppled backward. I tried to grab her, but my poisoned body wouldn't move. Her shadow flickered out. *Allie!*

Motion blurred around me. Nearby, Elin. Farther off, some wild gray creature slower than the owl. I heard cloth tear as Elin pulled the owl from my shoulders and tossed it, lifeless, to the black stone. A gray muzzle nudged my face. *Matthew.* I couldn't make my lips form his name. I couldn't remember why it was so important that he come. He moved from me to nudge Allie, but she didn't move. Elin crouched beside them.

Matthew threw back his head and howled. Caleb ran to his side, wearing an oilskin cloak and nylon pack. It was important that Caleb come, too. He knelt by Allie, his face grim, while Elin took the pack from his shoulders. He put his hands to Allie's chest. Silver light bloomed, then flickered out as surely as her shadow had. Matthew whined. Caleb moved toward me. I saw his hands reach for my shoulders and back, felt a searing wave of fire. I found voice at last to scream as more silver flashed around me.

Numbness left my limbs, my thoughts. I rolled away from Caleb as the fire burned on. "Not me—Allie! It's Allie who needs you!"

Caleb grabbed my wrists, flesh and stone, pulling me up to sitting. I fought him. Matthew gave a sharp bark.

"Liza!" Caleb didn't let go. "If I do not heal you, *you cannot call her back!*"

His words washed over me like cold river water.

Shadow. Allie had no shadow. Caleb couldn't heal anyone without a shadow.

Only a summoner could call shadows back from the dead.

I slumped in his hold. Caleb returned his hands to my shoulders and back. Healing cold flowed through my wounds. Matthew leaned his head on my leg with a sigh. I dug my fingers into his ruff. There were orange leaves in his fur and a long scratch down one side of his nose.

Elin remained by Allie. Behind them, the first hints of gray touched the sky. "She killed the owl," the weaver said. "To save you."

There's only two times it's okay to kill with healing magic. When someone is in pain and when someone's causing it. Allie had used her magic on the owl, the magic that had already made her so ill. She'd pushed too hard at last, and she'd—

No. Caleb wouldn't have spoken of calling her back if there wasn't hope of saving her. His healing magic flared with a final icy gust and was gone, leaving me gasping. I released Matthew and crawled over to Allie. Her arms were spread wide, and there was a small smile on her face. I touched her brow. It was warm, as if her body didn't know her shadow was gone. Matthew looked up at me, sorrow in his wolf's eyes.

I wasn't helpless, not now. My magic could yet set this right.

"Careful, Liza." Caleb's voice was stretched taut. "Do nothing you cannot do safely."

"Allie!" I *would* set this right. I would protect her like I'd promised. *"Allison! Come here!"*

No answer. I called on all my magic, all my power. *"Allison! Come back!"* My voice rang through the growing dawn.

Some memory of shadow flickered beside her, like a wick reluctant to catch. *"Allison!"*

Something stirred deep within me. *"Come here,"* the River called to me in turn. *"Seek sleep, seek darkness, seek rest."* Its voice urged me toward the depths and the gray. The seeds in my pocket fought that pull once more, urging me to the surface, toward sun and growth and light.

If I moved toward the light, I would lose her. *"Allison!"* The flickering shadow gained strength, took on shape: a gray girl in a loose nightgown, looking down at her physical body as if it were strange to her.

"Go to her," the River said.

Of course I wanted to go to her. I reached for Allie's shadow hand with my flesh one. Her hand passed right through mine, and ice knifed up my arm. Allie drew back from me like a wary cat. I reached for her with my stone hand, but her shadow passed through that as well.

I'd held shadows before. What had I done when I'd held them?

I looked down at my hands. I had a shadow, too. I just couldn't see it. A healer couldn't heal herself, and a summoner couldn't see or command her own shadow. Not anymore—but once, long ago, Rhianne had sent her shadow far beyond her body.

I didn't need to go as far as Rhianne had. I needed only to go the very slightest distance beyond my own skin. I unfocused my gaze the way Karin taught me when I first learned to see shadows, and I stared down at my own hands.

I saw flesh and stone, nothing more. I closed my eyes, remembering the life I'd felt within my stone hand when Nys touched it, life I could not see. I reached for the tingling warmth of his touch, fighting the sick feeling it churned up, focusing on the stirring of life—of shadow—within stone. *"Allison."* Something shuddered awake within my hand. I reached out with that something, reached out and touched Allie's hand. My stone fingers, dead no longer, wrapped around hers. Allie's hand was cold, but the cold didn't trouble me now.

"Liza!" Caleb's voice seemed very far away. A faint musty smell drifted toward me.

"So you see," the River said. *"It is not so hard as it seems."*

I felt a shiver of fear at that voice, even as Allie pulled on my hand, trying to get away from me.

I didn't let go. "Allie. It's all right. It's me, Liza. *Come here.*"

"You can't," Allie whispered. "You can't follow me, or it will all have been for nothing."

What did she mean, follow her? I opened my eyes. Allie looked up at me. She was as solid and real as I was, only drained of all color, hair and nightgown and boots cast in shades of gray, despair and anger mixed in her colorless eyes. I looked down at our linked hands. No stone weighed me down now, but my living hands and all the rest of me were the same shades of gray as Allie. I hadn't called her back. I'd slipped into shadow with her instead. We stood together on a dead, gray plain. I knew this place. It was the place things went when they died. I'd been here before.

There were no clouds, no bright moon. Silence weighed on me, urging me to my knees, strong as any glamour, but the seeds I held spoke to something deeper within me, reminding me of color and light. I remained standing.

Allie kept trying to pull away. "Let me *go.*" Her voice was at the edge of hearing, as if sound had no more place here than color.

I braced against the gray ash at our feet. She'd begged me to let her go with Nys once, too.

"You don't understand." Allie twisted in my hold, kicking up a cloud of stale dust. "I have to go, but you have a choice. I saved you, only you won't let yourself be saved. Please, Liza. There are people who need you back there." Her seed must have been speaking to something in her, too, if she could fight me. I'd never been able to fight anything in the gray place before.

Ashes drifted back to the ground. Allie sagged in my hold, then abruptly aimed a kick at my shin. Her foot connected. The pain was muted, as if we fought wrapped in feathers, but its weight knocked me back. Allie broke free, and she ran.

I chased her over the empty plain, knowing she ran toward sleep, toward death. *"Allison. Stop."* The gray softened my command as surely as it had softened Allie's kick, but she skidded to a halt. I grabbed her, and she went limp in my arms. I turned back the way we'd come—the way I thought we'd come. The gray looked the same in every direction, and I saw no way out.

"Liza. Please." Allie voice caught. "It *hurts* not to answer the call. Let me go."

Healing did hurt sometimes—I didn't know how to heal. I only knew how to call things to me, to send them away. I only knew how to hold on.

That's what I would do, then. I set Allie down, grabbing her hand as I did. "All right. Show me where we need to go."

She began pulling against me again, pulling hard. The stale smell grew stronger, taking on a sickly sweetness.

I wouldn't leave her alone in the dark. I was the one who stopped fighting to follow where she led, deeper into the gray.

～ *Chapter 12* ～

"Liza, no." Allie's feet crunched softly over the ash.

I matched her steady pace. Whatever call she answered, I did not feel it. "I won't try to stop you, if this is what you need to do. But I won't leave you, either."

Allie sighed, the nearest thing to wind in this dead place. "What did I ever bother healing you for if you were only going to do this?"

"I always was a terrible patient." I managed a strangled laugh.

"Liza! That's not funny." But Allie laughed, too, a laugh that caught on something like a hiccup. "What about Matthew? He'll never forgive you for this."

He would, though. That was the worst part. Matthew understood risking oneself for others as well as I did. Allie, too, I realized. Struggling to save what we could, it was what we all *did*. If I didn't come back, Matthew would only regret that he couldn't save me in turn.

I wasn't giving up on saving myself or Allie just yet. I scanned the empty land as I followed her, looking for any change, any hint of a way out. Gray weighed at my steps. A breath of cold brushed my ankle, and a shapeless shadow floated past. Something in that shadow called to me and my magic, longing to be laid to rest.

Even here? I'd thought this was where shadows found rest when I sent them away.

The seeds I carried still called to me, too. I drew one into my free hand. Its husk seemed faint, not as real as the shadow within it. It had been a seed found in the gray that had shown me the way out the first time I was here. That seed had become my quia tree. Could this seed, which came from my tree in turn, also show us a way out?

"*Grow.*" My voice—my magic—came out as a whisper. "*Seek sun, seek sky, seek life.*"

The seed's shadow began to unfurl. A flash of green filled my sight.

"*Stop!*" A woman's voice echoed around us. "*Seek silence, seek stillness, seek sleep!*" Allie and I staggered beneath the power in her command. The seed shuddered, and its shadow curled back up. Just like that.

The voice had come from the direction Allie was

walking. A summoner's voice, one with more power than mine. I slowed my steps as I returned the seed to the others, forcing Allie to slow as well. "Show yourself," I said. The gray swallowed my words, leaving behind the barest of whispers.

Laughter rustled over the land, like wind through fallen leaves, no joy in it. "That is one thing I cannot do." Whoever this summoner was, the gray didn't mute her voice. "You must come to me, as all who walk here do, soon or late."

I shivered, not from cold. Allie pulled me on, toward the voice. At least this enemy—if she was an enemy—was not at our backs. More shadows drifted past, as if on some unfelt wind. I sensed longing from them all; if they sought sleep, they were not finding it. So many. My eyes stung, but when I brought my arm to my face, it was dry, as if tears had no place in the gray.

The shadows thickened into a chill tide. Some held hints of their former shapes: a grasping hand, an outstretched paw, a leafy branch. It wasn't only humans whose shadows came here when they died.

Something dark loomed out of the gray. A tree's thick roots, taller than I was, disappearing into the ashes below me, merging into a thick trunk that stretched out of view far above. Shadows drifted toward the roots from all directions, swirling around them with a soupy thickness. The air grew heavy, as it did before a storm, but my throat felt dry as a summer without rain.

"No!" Allie jerked to a stop less than an arm's length from the tree. She pounded at a root, but her hand went right through it, as if the tree were more real than she was. "No no no no *no*." This tree wasn't a shadow. It *had* a shadow, deep within it, as Allie and I did not.

"It isn't *fair*." Allie looked up past the roots, to the tree's broad trunk. "I need to leave, but there's nowhere to go." She tugged at my hand, more desperately. "Why?"

"You could release the seeds you carry." The woman's voice came from the tree, gentler this time. "It would be easier for you if you did."

I looked more closely at the tree's shadow and saw hints of legs within its roots, hints of a woman's body within its trunk. Woman and tree, tangled together as surely as wolf and boy were tangled in Matthew. I knew her then, knew her as the same woman whose arms were tangled within this tree's shadow branches in Faerie. The First Tree's roots truly had gone deep.

"Rhianne," I said.

"Indeed." Somewhere up out of sight, wind rattled dry branches, but I did not feel it. "How do you come to be here, little summoner, knowing my true name while holding your own name close, carrying green life to the heart of death itself? You feel familiar. You have been here before."

"We didn't mean to be here," I said. "We'd gladly leave, if only you'd show us the way."

"You so lightly seek what those around you cannot have? A return to light and life?"

"Not me. I know it's over for me." Allie took her own seed in her hand. "If I let go of this, will I be free?" The longing in her eyes felt colder than any gray. It was the same longing I sensed from the drifting shadows all around us.

"No," Rhianne said, sorrow in her voice. "You will not be free. But you will no longer know it, for when you let the seed go, you let your name go as well. There will be an end to pain, to the knowledge of suffering."

"But not to the suffering itself?" Allie kept staring at the seed.

"All things lose their names when they come here," Rhianne said. "Some gradually, as they cling to matters left unfinished in the living world, some swiftly, if their work in that world is done. But by the time they reach this tree, they've let the memory of who they are go. All except you."

"It hurts." Allie looked small and forlorn as a figure seen through falling snow. "Like a hole, deep inside me."

I tightened my grip on her. "Let us out of here, and we won't trouble you anymore. You have my word."

More laughter, even as Rhianne asked, "*What is your name?*"

Almost, my lips parted at her command. Almost, I answered her question. "She's a summoner," I reminded Allie. Rhianne would have power over us if we gave her our names.

"This is wrong." Allie's gaze swept over the shadows flowing around Rhianne's tree. "They shouldn't be here. I shouldn't be here. Whatever happens next—and no one knows what happens next, not even healers—it isn't supposed to be this."

"My roots hold them here," Rhianne said.

"So uproot them," Allie said.

"Would you condemn all my children up above?" An edge crept into Rhianne's voice, reminding me of Nys when we'd asked him to set Tolven free. "Though many perished in the burning, some live on in the bright world, safe from death. My own daughter is among them."

Her daughter? "Mirinda's dead," I said. Elin had said so. *In time Mirinda passed from the Realm.*

A sharp crack, like lightning splitting a tree, echoed somewhere deep inside me. I stumbled, almost lost my hold on Allie.

"My daughter is not here." The ice in Rhianne's

voice made Nys seem kind after all. "I would know if she were. Yet she'll not remain safe long if my roots release their hold on the gray. The seeds my people ate will lose their power without my roots and my magic behind them. Only this tree stands between the living world and the unknown dark beyond this place. If I let go, within a few short years all my people will slip into that dark. If protecting them from death means holding on to those shadows that do come here, I accept that price."

"I don't accept it!" Allie stamped her foot, but it made no sound. "We're *supposed* to slip into the unknown. That's what happens when we die."

"For those of lesser power, perhaps. But if my magic has strength enough to keep my people safe, I will use it."

"Is it only your people's shadows who are trapped here?" As soon as I asked, I knew it wasn't true. Allie wouldn't have been drawn to this tree if it was. I looked to the endless gray beyond trunk and roots. The shadows thinned, and somewhere past them a smaller tree stood, nothing human about it.

I thought of all my dead. My first sister. My cat. Kyle's older brother. Ethan's younger one. Strangers who'd died during the War or after it. I'd thought I'd laid their shadows to rest, but they weren't resting. They were drifting, nameless and lost, among the roots of this tree. My people paid the price of the faerie folks' long life, too, and we gained nothing from it.

The musty scent was stronger, so close to Rhianne's tree, the smell of gray dust. Did the crumbling come from here? The cost of Rhianne's gifts might be higher than we knew. "Faerie and my world both crumble away," I told Rhianne. "Is that part of the price you choose to pay, too?"

"Since the burning, the strain on the world is greater than it once was, it is true," Rhianne said. "Many shadows have flooded this place in a short time. I can handle that strain. For my people's sake I'll hold on, so that they can endure as long as they may."

"You don't understand!" Allie said, and I realized it was true. Two worlds were crumbling because Rhianne and her roots stood here holding back death, and she only wanted to hold on harder. I couldn't let her do that.

I knew her name. Could I make her roots let the gray go and so set all the shadows free? Would that be enough to make the crumbling stop as well? Allie was staring at her seed again. I wasn't sure I could both save her and make Rhianne let go.

I couldn't let this stand just to protect Allie and me. Some part of me wanted to, though.

Best to act swiftly, then, before I could change my

mind. *"Rhianne! Go away!"* With all my magic behind the words, I forced them past a whisper, into a squeaking command. The roots trembled. *"Go away, go away, go away!"*

The ground lurched, an earthquake that threw me from my feet. I clutched Allie's hand as we fell, though she fought to pull free once more. Shadows blurred, and something in the gray air seemed to give, like rope gone slack, letting a flash of green through.

"How dare you!" The shadows snapped back into focus with a sound like ripping cloth, and the green was gone. *"Your name, Summoner."* There was power in Rhianne's words, too, harsh power that coiled around me, with none of glamour's illusions.

"Liza." The name slid too easily from my lips. I tried to draw breath, to take it back, but I couldn't.

"Go, Liza!" Rhianne's call rippled through my shadow and my thoughts, reminding me how fragile they were. *"Distract me from my work here no longer, lest you hasten that which you seek to prevent. Go!"* My vision dimmed. *"Take your name back to the world with you. Return to me in your own time, when your body and shadow fail, when your name and your power are lost. Go!"* My shadow frayed like old yarn as the darkness took me, the very fibers of my being pulling, pulling apart, my hold on Allie weakening as they did.

Silver flashed at the edges of my sight, but it was too far. My shadow was unraveling, letting emptiness through.

I felt an uncomfortable *tug*, and then something gathered up the fraying threads of my being. With a gasp I shuddered into skin and bone, while the something wove the threads back together—too tight. I screamed, blinking to see silver eyes staring down at me, wide, startled. Elin. She crouched across from me beneath a blue sky, on the other side of Allie's body, one hand resting on Allie's chest, the other touching my shoulder.

For just a moment the shivering air between us seemed made, not of air and sky, but of shimmering silver fibers. "What I felt—what I wove—no one can weave—" Elin shuddered and toppled to the ground.

Allie lurched upright, looked at me, and began to cry.

∽ *Chapter 13* ∼

Matthew was at Elin's side, human now, pressing his fingers against her neck. He must have found a pulse, because he let out a long sigh. Caleb knelt before Allie, grasping her trembling shoulders. Silver threads flowed from his hands and wove themselves into a web. The web disappeared beneath Allie's skin, but her shaking didn't ease. "The radiation sickness wasn't as advanced as I'd feared," Caleb said gravely.

Elin stirred. Matthew looked at me as he helped her sit up.

I was trembling, too. My skin felt thin as paper from Before. "I'm all right." My fingers—my stone fingers—were wrapped around Allie's. She tried to pull free, but the stone held tight. Caleb pried her fingers loose, one by one, a strange look on his face. I glanced down at my hand. It was clenched in a tighter fist than before, tight enough to have held Allie's smaller hand. When my shadow had moved, the stone had moved as well.

Elin pressed her hands up to her face. "I can see them. In the air, all around us—the threads of the world. I've always felt them, but I could not see them. No weaver can see them." She shivered in the cloak that was again wrapped around her, its edges now trimmed with owl feathers. I remembered the shimmer of silver fibers. I felt something of that still, a shiver in the air that echoed beneath my skin.

Allie kept crying. She was here. I'd brought her back, and Caleb had healed her. Those were the important things. Matthew moved to my side, and I wrapped my arms around him, burying my face against his shoulder, smelling the wolf in his hair, feeling my stone hand weighing me down once more.

Matthew rubbed my back. "You were gone so long."

"How long?" I drew away and ran my finger down Matthew's cheek, where a long cut was clotted with dried blood.

"A day and a half." He wore Caleb's quia leaf over his sweater. That leaf would protect Matthew from glamour, but if it was hurt in any way, Caleb would be hurt, too.

It hadn't seemed a day and a half in the gray. Yet the

sky was clear, the sun just beginning its descent. I saw the remains of a fire—Elin's glowing stone must have run out—beside a woodpile and a few cracked bones that were all that remained of the owl.

"Someone had to eat it." Matthew shrugged, as if embarrassed, but his expression went bleak. "You were still breathing. That's the only reason we didn't give up. But Allie wasn't breathing, Liza, and her heart wasn't beating. Caleb kept her body from decay, just in case, but none of us really believed—" Matthew grasped my wrist, where stone gave way to flesh. "I thought I'd lost you."

He almost had lost me. If I'd sent Rhianne away and set the shadows free, he would have lost me. If Elin hadn't done whatever it was she'd done, he'd have lost me even after I returned. I tucked a strand of hair back into his ponytail. Around us, I saw patches of gray forest that hadn't been there before. Elin had surely warned Caleb about the border protections by now. The rest of us needed to get back to Karin.

A few evening crickets began to chirr. Matthew shoved a piece of dried deer meat into my hands. I chewed mechanically, barely tasting it. It was Rhianne we needed to get back to. We had to make her tree let go, or the crumbling would go on and on.

Elin continued staring at her hands. Allie kept crying.

Caleb made calming sounds as he ran his hands over her. I tried to meet Allie's eyes; she flinched and turned away. "Sorry," she whispered, to Caleb, not to me. "But it hurts so much."

Caleb had healed Allie, hadn't he? He glanced at me. "Liza. I need to know. How far did you go to find her?"

Beyond the crossroads, the setting sun lit the edges of the autumn leaves with fire. "To the tree." I reached for Matthew with my good hand, drawing him close. I needed warmth, light, life. I needed to know I'd gone far enough to save her.

"Hurts." Allie's tears turned to shuddering sobs. I'd never seen her cry like this. "Make it— Can you make it stop, Caleb?" The fading light made her shadow seem too thin, as if some strand had been left out of its weaving.

"What tree?" Caleb asked me.

"Rhianne's tree," I said.

Elin dropped her hands into her lap. "That," she said flatly, "is impossible. We're not even sure the First Tree's roots reach that far."

"I think we're sure now." Caleb lifted a rock—more flint—and struck it against the ground. A chip of stone flaked away, and he sliced it across his thumb, drawing blood. "Heal this," he told Allie.

Allie swallowed and reached for his hand. Their

fingers touched, and then she jerked back as if burned, burying her head in her hands. "I can't. It's gone."

What was gone? Her magic? Magic couldn't just be gone.

Caleb's face was pale in the fading light. "That is where the pain comes from. You were too far into death when Liza found you. She brought as much of you back as she could, but she couldn't bring back everything. Our magic and our names are the first things we lose."

The night was growing cold. Matthew piled kindling for a fire. I should have helped him, but I kept staring at Caleb and Allie. Elin did the same.

"I knew it was too late. I knew, but Liza—" Allie looked at me, looked away.

I hadn't been strong enough. I'd failed her after all.

"Can you fix it, Caleb?" Allie's voice seemed as thin as her shadow.

Caleb's silver gaze grew distant. "There is a thing that may help. But it is not an easy thing. And you will not thank me for it, not for a long time."

"I'm not afraid of pain." Allie's eyes glistened in the dimness. "You know I'm not. I just need to know it won't be forever, that's all."

"I can offer you sleep, to start with," Caleb said. "If you will accept it."

"Yes." Allie nodded vigorously. "Please."

Pain flashed across Caleb's face. Matthew's flint sparked. Tinder caught, smoldered. Caleb put his hands gently to Allie's temples, and Allie lay back on the stones with a sigh.

Light flashed beneath his hands. Allie shuddered, then smiled, like a child dosed with whiskey against pain. "Oh, that's better. I can still feel it, but I don't care so much." She closed her eyes. We waited while Matthew fed small sticks to the fire and Allie's breath began to slow into sleep.

Her breath sped up again, grew uneven. She squeezed her eyes shut more tightly, and tears leaked from them. "Not enough." Her voice rasped. Caleb frowned and put his hands to her chest. Allie bolted upright, screaming. "Too much! Too much is missing! I can't—" She shuddered violently. Caleb grasped her shoulders, trying to still her.

She fought him, convulsing in his hold. My heart pounded. Matthew moved to my side, but I barely noticed. I needed to do something, anything. I couldn't lose Allie now.

Light flowed like a blanket from Caleb's hands, wrapping around her. Allie went limp as the light faded, but she didn't stop screaming. "I can't! So empty—send me back, Caleb. There's not enough of me left. You have to send me back!"

Caleb laid her gently on the stones. Her motionless body was at odds with her cries. Caleb must have frozen her limbs. He'd fix this. He had to fix this. My chest hurt, as if a piece of me were missing, too. Allie never should have killed that owl, not for me.

"I will make this right," Caleb whispered. "You have my word."

Matthew's fire wasn't enough to keep away the chill. "How will you make it right?" I demanded. "By healing her or killing her?"

"It doesn't matter," Allie whimpered.

Matthew shivered, though he was nearer the fire than me. "It does matter," he said.

"Without the magic, there's nothing left." Allie's cries gave way to ragged wheezing.

"Breathe, Allison." Caleb pushed Allie's hair back from her face. "As I taught you. You can breathe through this."

Allie shut her eyes, as if breathing took work. The flow of air in and out of her chest deepened. "I can't do this," she whispered.

"You can, and you will." Caleb moved her arms to her sides. "You are more than your magic. You always have been. You always will be."

Allie continued to take ragged breaths. Her eyes remained shut against pain I could not see. She wouldn't have been in pain if I'd let go her hand.

Caleb turned to me. "If this does not go as expected, Liza, there must be no calling of anyone back from the dead. Not this time."

A wind picked up, blowing smoke toward us. "Was I wrong to bring her back?"

"I do not know." The smoke drifted past Caleb's face, obscuring his expression. "I only know I'd have done the same, had I your power. But I need your word you will not use that power now, no matter what happens. I know it is a hard thing I ask. I do not ask it lightly."

He wanted me to let Allie go if he couldn't save her. He wanted me to promise not to call her back again. Smoke made my eyes sting. I'd done all I could. I would have to trust Caleb to do all he could in turn and to know when nothing more could be done. "You have my word. I will not use my summoning here." I swallowed. "Do we need to take away her seed?" If Caleb failed, would it be better to let Allie go with her name or without it?

"One of your quia seeds?" Caleb asked. The wind shifted, taking the smoke away.

I nodded and drew a seed from my pocket to show him. "Allie has one, too. With the seeds, we were able to hold on to our names in the gray."

Caleb took the seed in his hands, and I saw a strange sort of hope in his eyes. "Allison. You carry a seed as well. Do you wish to keep it?"

Allie's eyes took a moment to focus on him. "Yes. Please." There was blood on her lip. She'd been biting it.

"You have others?" Caleb asked me. I nodded—there were two more in my pocket—and Caleb said, "May I keep this one, then? To study as I may?"

"Of course." Could he feel the life in it as Allie could?

"Elianna has told me much of what happened in Faerie." Caleb gave his niece a long look. She returned it, and I couldn't read what passed between them. "She has also told me why I cannot return there. I know well enough I ought to tell you not to return, either, but I'll not deny I'm glad you can go where I cannot. If I can restore Allison's magic to her, she should be able to render my sister senseless long enough to get her free, if only she can get close enough."

"Like you did," I said. In my vision, Caleb had used his magic to make Karin fall unconscious. Matthew piled thicker branches on the fire. Orange flames licked the night.

"Like I did," Caleb agreed. He slipped the seed into his pocket. "One more thing I can give to you: Nysraneth's name." Something dark crossed his face. "In abusing my student, my father has forfeited all right for me to hold that name safe."

Allie bit her lip harder, making it bleed more freely.

Caleb put his hands to her chest. "You are Allison. You are my student. I will not leave you like this."

The crickets chirred, loud in the night. I reached for Matthew's hand, hoping, afraid to hope. Elin bunched her hands in the skirt of her dress.

Light sparked beneath Caleb's hands, green-gold, restless as summer lightning. I felt its heat against my skin, nothing like the silver chill of most magic. This was the warmth of dawn, of sunlight, of life.

Elin made a sharp sound. The green-gold light spread through Allie's body, like spilled water through parched soil. Bone shone through skin, everything about her turned to light. Her breathing steadied, and a smile crossed her face, the first smile I'd seen from her since we returned from Faerie.

Caleb's arms stiffened against her, and he smiled, too, but there was sorrow in it. "Forgive me, Tara."

What? Why—

Allie's eyes shot open. "Caleb, no!"

He crumpled on top of her, and his shadow flickered out.

⌣ *Chapter 14* ⌣

"Smoke and ash," Elin hissed. Matthew and I rolled Caleb over, Allie putting her hands to his chest as Matthew felt for a pulse. I knew from both their faces—from the way Caleb's silver eyes stared up at the night sky, from the way my own eyes saw no shadow within him— what they found.

Kaylen! His name stuck in my throat. *You have my word,* I'd said. *I will not use my summoning here.* It wasn't Allie he'd been afraid I'd call back from the dead. It was himself. My heart pounded, like a wild thing trying to get free. Of course I had to call him back. Yet my promise bound me. I couldn't get his name past my lips. "He knew," I whispered. "He knew this would happen."

"Of course he knew." Elin's voice was rough as coarse-spun wool. "My people do not do things by accident as yours do. I do not understand this sacrifice, but I will not have you diminish it by deeming it a mistake."

The fire was burning down, leaving behind a cold, cloudless night, but no one moved to feed it. I was cold, too, cold and numb. Matthew clutched the leaf he wore. It crumbled to silver dust in his hand. Caleb was truly gone, beyond the reach of any of our magics.

Allie's hands remained on his chest. "You never asked, Caleb. If I wanted this! You're the one who taught me you're always supposed to ask." She looked up at me, tears streaming down her face. "Why doesn't anyone ever *ask*?"

My throat hurt. I wasn't sure I'd ever find words again. "I'm—" I couldn't tell Allie I was sorry she wasn't dead. I reached for her instead.

She jerked away, staggering to her feet. "Don't."

"Don't what?" I was on my feet, too. Beside me, Matthew quietly closed Caleb's eyes, getting silver dust on the healer's lids. There was more dust on Matthew's sweater and hands. It shimmered like starlight in the growing dark.

Allie's eyes were wild. She whirled from us and fled, across the stone and into the forest. Matthew and I exchanged a glance and ran after her. A ragweed shadow snaked out from among the trees to wrap around Allie's thigh. She fell to the forest floor.

"*Go away!*" I hissed at the shadow, and it withdrew. I knelt to press my hands to Allie's leg. It was sticky with blood.

"Leave me alone!" Allie shoved my hands away. "You never know when to leave anything alone!"

Matthew lifted his head, as if at some scent. Something stale drifted toward us. Just behind Allie, dust trickled from a poplar tree to the forest floor. Behind it, a patch of darkness crept toward us.

"Allie." I whispered my warning.

"Don't talk to me!"

"You need to come back with us, Allie. The crumbling—"

"I don't care!" Allie beat the dirt like a much younger child. "If the crumbling takes me, everything will be over, like it's supposed to be, and even you won't be able to change that."

Another trickle of dust. I wanted to hit and kick and scream at things, too, but we couldn't afford that, not now.

Matthew knelt to touch Allie's shoulder. "Dying won't bring him back."

Allie didn't push him away, not like she had me. "I know that, I do, but—" She looked up at him, eyes bright.

Matthew reached out his hand, and Allie took it.

"This will never be right," she said. "Never, never, never."

"I know." Matthew led her back to where Caleb lay, but I just kept staring into the forest. If I'd noticed the owl sooner—if I'd fought Nys off better—if I'd called Allie back sooner—I watched as the branches of the poplar crumbled away, one by one, and color drained out of the world. Behind me, I heard Allie's sobs, heard Matthew making shushing sounds, but that seemed far away, nothing to do with me.

Forgive me, Tara. The darkness sank down into the soil, leaving behind a bare trunk, but color did not return to the world. The last of the sun was gone. How could I ever tell Mom about this?

There'd be no one to help her if anything went wrong with the baby now.

I returned to the others. Of course I did. I could no more let the crumbling take me than the rest of them, if I had a choice.

Matthew had bound Allie's leg where the ragweed shadow had touched her. She ran a finger along his cheek as she chewed on some dried meat. Silver light traced the ragged cut there, and then the cut was gone. "It's back. My magic. It's back, and I'm fine, and—" She looked back to Caleb. "What did you *do*?"

"He gave you his magic." Elin knelt at Caleb's feet,

not moving. By the dying firelight, her face and Caleb's looked equally pale. Once before, Caleb had nearly died of a healing, but I'd called him back. Calling him back had been right then. How could it have become so wrong, so fast?

"It is a thing we can do." Elin's voice was hard and pitiless. "To share our power. You should know that, Liza. My mother shared her magic with you when you called back spring. It is meant to be a brief thing: a loaning of magic, not a gift. If Kaylen and Allie's magics weren't the same, he never could have given his power away so completely."

Matthew blew on the fire. Red coals glowed, returned to gray. *"Come here,"* I whispered to the fire, but it didn't listen to me. I could no more call heat from coals than I could call Caleb's cold body to life. What was the point of my magic if it couldn't bring back those I cared for? Only Rhianne's magic could hold back death—but that was wrong, too, so wrong.

A soft sound escaped my lips. Matthew abandoned the fire to grab my wrists. "Liza. You know this isn't your fault, don't you?"

"Tell Allie that. Tell Caleb." I knew no such thing.

Matthew tightened his grip on flesh and stone. "Blame the owl. Blame radiation poisoning. Blame—" He glanced at Elin. She looked right back, no apology there. "Blame the goddamn War if you have to. Just don't—don't—" Matthew leaned his head on my shoulder. He was trembling. So was I. His face brushed the side of my neck. "It's awful," he said. "That's all."

"That is *not* all." Elin stood as we pulled apart, anger in her every movement. "It is Liza's fault. It is all your faults. You die so easily, so soon—in a season you will all be gone, and this death will be for nothing. That one of us should die for one of you—nothing can make that right."

"That's not what Caleb thought." Allie's voice was strangely calm, as if she'd yelled herself out. "He never believed we were worth less because we were human." She reached into Caleb's pocket and drew out the quia seed he'd taken from me. I saw no shadow in the seed, felt no green life within it, though the seeds in my pocket and Allie's still lived.

"Dead." Allie flung the empty seed away. She bent over Caleb, tangled hair hiding her face. "If you have to be trapped," she whispered to him, "I hope you at least get to keep your name."

Matthew blew on the fire again, but this time no light came to the coals. I shivered. Caleb would be trapped by Rhianne's tree as surely as we had been. Wherever he was supposed to go next, he would no more be able to get there than Allie had.

"I would never have woven your shadows back into this world," Elin whispered, "had I known it would come to this."

Was that what Elin had done? The thought was a distant one. Matthew stirred the fire with a dead branch, but the coals remained dead. How could a fire die so fast? Matthew stopped stirring abruptly as I caught a scent beneath that of the smoke, the scent of something stagnant and old. Matthew lifted the branch, and half of it crumbled away, back into the fire. He dropped the wood. It wasn't burning that had put this fire out.

The crickets had fallen silent. We both took a few steps back, toward Elin and Allie and Caleb. The stagnant scent came from behind us, too. Up above, the black sky held no stars. It was too dark; I couldn't tell how near the crumbling was. I could only smell it. The wind shifted, and I caught it from a third direction, too. "We need light."

"You truly cannot see." Elin turned in a slow circle. "Your people have always seen less well than mine. Let me make it easy for you, then. We are surrounded. There is no way out."

✎ *Chapter 15* ❧

I strained to see into the dark. Were there fewer trees at the edge of the clearing than before? I couldn't tell. I slammed my flesh fist into my stone one, breaking skin. Allie shuddered as I held out my stinging knuckles. "Can you heal this?"

She finally met my eyes. "Don't you ever do that again." Anger burned in her gaze, and I knew she knew why I asked. She pressed her fingers to mine. There was a shimmer of silver light, too dim to show anything but Allie's face and both our hands, and then it and the stinging were both gone.

"I could have told you it wouldn't be enough light to see by." Allie bent back over Caleb. "I never want to hurt anyone if I can help it. You ought to know that by now."

Matthew had found a branch untouched by the fire and its crumbling. He knelt as he shredded its bark into tinder. *"Go away,"* I whispered into the dark, but it remained as thick as before. I scanned it for any hint of light.

Silver flickered at the corners of my sight, like some faint magic. When I turned to it, it was gone.

I turned away again, unfocusing my gaze, willing the flicker to return. I saw faint silver fibers, shining through the emptiness, the same shimmering threads I'd seen between Elin and me when I'd returned from the gray, thin as nylon thread.

Nylon thread was stronger than it seemed. Still not looking at the threads directly, I called, *"Come here."*

The fibers flared brighter, shivered, and flowed toward me. By their light, I saw the darkness and dust that hovered all around us, the dead fire and Caleb's backpack half swallowed by it, no gap large enough for us to get through. I grabbed the silver strands into my outstretched hand, as if carding light out of the dark. So cold that light—I gasped as I swiftly wrapped the bright fibers around my stone fist, which couldn't feel the cold, wrapped them around it as surely as a weaver wrapped unspun wool around a distaff.

I wasn't a weaver. I held my hand out to Elin.

"The threads of the world." Her voice was so strange

I didn't at first recognize what I heard in it: wonder. "You feel them, too."

I didn't feel them, not as I felt the life in trees and people and shadows. But I saw, in the pulsing fibers, something more alive than simple light, something with a spirit of its own.

Matthew had stopped shredding the bark. He and Allie both stared at us. Elin kept staring, too.

"Can you use this?" I looked at Elin, at the crumbling all around us. "Against the dark?"

Elin's eyes grew wide. Then, in a voice like a slow smile, "I can indeed." She thrust her hands into the light I held, running her fingers through it, aligning fibers to pull them together into thicker strands. Cold brushed my face, and my breath came out in icy puffs. Elin drew the bright strands from my stone hand, which was rimed with frost, and she kept running her hands through that light, like a shuttle through a loom. Light stretched and grew, as a weaving on a frame, into a rectangle of bright silver light. I caught the faint winter scent of the sky before snow as Elin walked to the edge of the darkness. That darkness gathered and bunched, retreating from the light she held. She set it down, like a shining doorway, and then she plunged her hands into it once more, pushing threads aside, leaving the doorway open into the night. Through it, I heard the faint chirr of crickets.

Elin was shivering, but she didn't seem to notice. A wry smile tugged at her face. "That should do well enough." By the silver light, everything about her seemed to glow.

Matthew got to his feet. "I don't know what the two of you did. But that was—amazing." He tried to pull Allie to her feet as well.

Allie remained crouched by Caleb's side. "We can't leave him here."

He wasn't here, not anymore. Surely Allie knew that as well as me. Before I could argue, though, Matthew crouched to lift Caleb's body over his shoulders. He walked through the doorway, and after a moment Allie followed. I went next. The stars on the other side shone so brightly, after the dark.

Elin went last, stopping on the other side to plunge her hand into the threads. "*Return to the world from which you came,*" she whispered, and the doorway gave way to shimmering fibers that dissolved into the night. She laughed softly, bitterly. "So you see, Grandmother. My power is not so small after all."

We followed the path downhill, toward Karin and the Arch, eager to put distance between ourselves and the crossroads. Elin led the way, and we let her, knowing she could see better than we could.

Knowing she had just saved our lives.

The crumbling was thicker than when we'd climbed up, and we had to wind our way on and off the path, around larger and larger patches of it. The living trees we ventured among held dangers of their own, but I kept their shadows away from us with my magic.

To our right, the River flowed steadily south. *"Liza,"* it whispered, *"you will not escape the dark for long. We shall meet again, and soon."* The water's voice held hints of another voice, Rhianne's voice, as if the River were a tear in the very world, one that let gray death through. Its pull was gentle now, easy enough to resist.

Allie pressed her lips together as she walked on; I couldn't tell if the River spoke to her or not. She was back to not looking at me. Matthew hunched a little under Caleb's weight. Where did we think we were taking him?

"We have no way to bury him." Anger darkened my words: at Allie for not wanting to be saved, at Caleb for saving her, at myself for not saving her sooner, so that none of this need have happened.

"Why would we bury him?" Allie lifted her chin. "Do they bury people in your town? Never mind—I know they do. But Caleb's not from your town, is he? We need to return him to the forest. That's what we do in *my* town."

"It is what my people do as well," Elin said quietly.

"Return him to the earth and the trees so that his body can become a part of life and growth once more."

"Exactly," Allie said.

I shivered as the path ended. From here there was only forest between us and the Arch. In my town we buried the dead, in hopes of keeping them from the grasping roots of the trees for as long as possible.

I looked to Matthew. Like me, he'd helped bury enough of those dead through the years. He just shrugged uneasily and said, "Would here do?"

Allie nodded, and she and Matthew followed Elin a few paces into the forest. I followed them in turn, continuing to keep the tree shadows at bay as I did. Matthew set Caleb down within a stand of river birches. Birches liked liquid, blood or water, it mattered little. We'd never leave anyone alone in such a place in our town, living or dead. I helped Matthew fold Caleb's hands over his heart. His skin was clammy and cold, like plastic drawn from a winter river.

I saw a chain disappearing beneath his sweater and took it from around his neck. The coin Mom had gifted him long ago hung there. I traced the Arch that was engraved upon it. The coin was a human thing and held no magic, but it endured where Caleb's leaf had not. I hung it around my own neck. Mom would want it.

Allie set something gently down beside Caleb: the

owl's skull. "Not the owl's fault it wanted to eat," she said.

A root broke through the earth and reached for Caleb's arm. *"Go—"* The word caught in my throat. The trees would take him soon enough. What was I trying to save? *"Go away!"* The root retreated into the earth.

Elin started to sing, a wordless song filled with the sounds of wild things: wind through weeds, rain on parched earth, a crow's beating wings, a running deer's feet as they hit the ground. Allie turned to her, eyes moist, and then she added a low hum of harmony to Elin's song. Elin blinked as if startled, but sang on.

Matthew and I exchanged a glance. We didn't know this song in our town. We had prayers, words about ashes and dust, but those were about death, and this song was about living things, growing things. It wasn't a human song—but Caleb and Karin must have thought it so, because who else could have taught it to Allie?

Abruptly Matthew raised his head, as if he smelled something. I didn't smell it, but Elin stopped singing. "I suggest we leave now," she said.

Dust trickled down one of the birches to land on Caleb's boot. In the faint starlight, I saw the boot begin crumbling away. We moved swiftly away through the trees, leaving Caleb behind. Matthew grabbed Allie's hand when she stopped to look back, pulling her on.

A whisper of stale air followed us all the way to the Arch. We moved to its base, as if it could provide protection. The stars were bright, a thin yellow moon just beginning to rise.

Matthew went very still. Elin's bright gaze fixed on him, and she drew her knife. "Don't move," she said. The stale scent came from right behind Matthew now. Elin stepped around him, cautious as a cat, to grab the top of his ponytail and slice the blade through it. Matthew stepped quickly forward, his remaining hair falling loose to brush his ears, as Elin dropped the hair she'd cut.

The moonlight was growing brighter. I saw clearly enough as Matthew's ponytail crumbled to dust. I pulled him into my arms. I was trembling, as if I'd been the one in danger of crumbling away.

"I didn't feel it. If I hadn't smelled it—" Matthew looked to Elin. "Thank you."

Elin turned away, as if uncomfortable, and gazed up the curve of the Arch instead. "You all remain pledged to help my mother?"

"You know we do," I said. We'd lost Caleb. I didn't intend to lose Karin, too, not if I could help it. We'd go back for her first, and then I'd figure out how to go after Rhianne again. Maybe Karin could help me try to stop her. "Elin told you all that happened?" I asked Matthew.

"When she told Caleb, yes." Matthew rubbed the back of his bare neck. "We had time."

"With time enough left over for Kaylen and Matthew to tell me just how great a fool I was," Elin said. "In considerable detail. They appeared to be under the misapprehension that I did not understand this already."

"The trees are supposed to remember him." Allie stared out into the night, as if none of us were there. "If they've all crumbled away, who will remember?"

"We'll have to do the remembering," I said. It seemed a small thing, and a great burden as well. I reached for Allie with my good hand, and this time, she let me take it.

Matthew took my stone hand in turn. He'd have no protection in Faerie, not with Caleb's leaf gone, and the seeds might not protect him, either, because there was nothing in his shifting magic that could sense the life within them.

I pulled away from them both to feel for the seeds in my pocket. Gifts of protection, but not for humans, not unless our own magic helped us. Even then our magic could only do so much. The true gifts were only for the faerie folk who ate these seeds long ago.

We didn't know that. I took a seed from my pocket, feeling its green life as I turned it between my fingers. There was only this seed and one more, plus the one

Allie held. If we ate them as Mirinda had, would Rhianne's gifts come to us, too? If they didn't, I'd lose what protection I had, but the risk might be worth it, for Matthew's and Allie's sake.

Elin's eyes narrowed. "Where did you get that? I saw a seed before, the one you gave Caleb. There was no chance to question you then."

"It's from my tree." I tightened my hold on the seed. Matthew moved close to me, sensing, as I did, the threat in Elin's tense stance.

"And what do you plan to do with this seed?" Her voice took on a hard edge.

No matter that she'd saved us, I doubted Elin would want us having the same protection as her people.

"Your intentions are not hard to guess," Elin said. "But you cannot imagine any quia seed would share its power with humans. It is deepest blasphemy for you even to hold one."

"What power?" Matthew asked.

I was tense, too, alert for any sudden move Elin might make. "Faerie power came from seeds like this."

"Like glamour?" Matthew rubbed the scar at his wrist.

"Not only casting glamour," I told him. "Protection from glamour, too. And seeing in the dark. Hearing over distances. Long life." It was long life, and the way Rhianne's hold on death stood behind it, that had brought this crumbling to us. I should want nothing to do with such things. Yet eating the seeds would not increase Rhianne's hold on death. That was already done, unless I found some way to undo it. If the quia seeds worked for us at all, they would merely grant us a share of the power whose price we were already paying.

"The seeds might well kill you," Elin said. "I would, before I'd share my power with a human."

"No, I don't think so." Allie turned back to us. "Not quickly, anyway." She held out her hands. By the moonlight, I saw broken pieces of shell. "Because if the seeds were going to kill us, I'd already be dead."

⤚⤳ Chapter 16 ⤛⤴

"Allie!" I looked her over for any sign of harm, but in the dark, I couldn't tell.

"Someone had to go first." Allie rubbed the pieces of shell off against her pants. "And if I'm going back to Faerie, I need to know I'll be safe this time. I can't have anyone taking me over, not ever again. Besides, if I'm going to live—and it's clear enough I am, because otherwise everything Caleb did would be wasted—the more protection I have, the better."

"How do you feel?" Matthew's face pinched with concern.

Allie smiled, a small, pleased smile. "Good. Really good."

"*What* do you feel?" The edge remained in Elin's voice.

Allie's smile grew. "I see colors, even though it's

nighttime. I feel small shifts in the ground beneath our feet. I hear—"

I saw the change in Elin's stance an instant before she lunged for the seed I held. We fell to the ground together as my sweater constricted, squeezing the air from my lungs. My sleeve constricted around my flesh hand, questing fibers trying to push between my fingers, to pry the seed free. Matthew leaped at us, shifting as he landed on Elin's back, fur flowing over his skin, teeth growing just in time to dig into her shoulder.

"*Elianna!*" I forced breath into my chest and my words. "*Stop!*"

Elin froze, my magic holding her. I pushed her to her feet as I stood. Matthew moved to sit beside her, snarling.

Allie brushed fingers along Elin's shoulder, which bled through her cloak. In a flash of silver light, the bleeding stopped. Elin's cloak fluttered restlessly about her, but otherwise she did not move. She could not move. My magic held her, a cold thread stretched taut between us. "It is rather convenient," she said, "that I have made vows not to harm you, but you have not once suggested you might offer similar vows in turn."

I used my teeth to tear my sweater free from around my fingers. "Would you deny us every last protection from your people?"

Elin gave a brittle laugh. "I stand trapped before you as surely as a cat in a tree, yet you continue to speak of *your* safety. Your people did much the same during the War. Do you think yourselves the only ones who know fear?"

I wouldn't forgo this protection just to make Elin feel safe. I slammed the seed against my stone hand. It cracked easily enough. Matthew growled, and his ears perked forward, a warning.

Elin couldn't stop me now. I used my teeth to peel the bits of shell away. The shell was bitter, but the seed within dissolved to syrupy sweetness as I chewed, sliding easily down my throat. I felt the green life in it still, but missed the exact moment when that life became part of me, adding its power to mine until I could no longer sense it, any more than I could sense my own shadow.

Color crept into the night world: the green of Elin's cloak, the red of Allie's hair, the brown of Matthew's pants and sweater where they lay on the ground. Matthew pressed his ears back against his head. Did he remain afraid the seeds would hurt us? "It's all right." I smelled damp earth, crisp leaves, droplets of water in the humid air, and behind it all a staleness that said none of this could last. I offered Matthew the final seed. He wouldn't care so much about the shell as a wolf.

He shook his head. Silver light flowed over gray fur,

and then he was human, shivering, gathering up his scattered clothes. I heard the chatter of his teeth, the River's steady flow, the soft breath of someone watching from the forest—the same watcher Elin had heard at the crossroads?

"You can let me go," Elin said. "It's too late for me to stop you."

Elin and our watcher would both have to wait. I kept holding the seed out to Matthew. I couldn't protect him from glamour, but the seed could. "I'm okay. Allie's okay. Truly." I felt fine. Better than fine.

"No." Matthew drew on pants and boots. There was a sheen of sweat on his chest. I smelled its salty tang.

Why would he refuse? I could see so much, smell so much. I felt stronger, more alert than I'd ever been. "Take it." I needed Matthew to take the seed. I needed him to be safe. "Please, Matthew." My words turned soft and urgent.

Something sleepy slid across Matthew's eyes. He reached slowly for the seed, as if he moved through deep water. Once he ate it, everything would be all right. He lifted the seed to his lips, but his soft eyes remained on me, his expression trusting as a child's.

The seed was in his mouth before I realized what was happening. "Stop!" I released the connection between us, a connection so subtle I hadn't felt it slide into place.

Matthew shuddered and spit the unbroken seed to the ground. It hadn't been him wanting to eat that seed. It'd been me, using glamour to make him do what I wanted. Elin threw back her head and laughed, the sound wild as an autumn storm. Our hidden listener's breathing slowed, as if to better watch us all.

The sleepy look had left Matthew's face, replaced by something more stark. Fear. "You don't want to make me do this, Liza."

I didn't—and I did. I wanted to protect him. Him most of all, of all those I sought to protect.

I glanced at Allie. Her eyes were wide, and I knew she understood what I'd almost done. I had precious little ability to protect anyone I cared for. The knowledge was cold and hard inside of me. I watched Matthew crush the seed beneath his boot. He didn't trust me, not with this.

I felt the spark of life in the seed flicker out. He was right not to trust me.

Elin kept laughing. "So you see, Liza. You are no better than us after all. We all seek power, and we all fear its lack."

Matthew flung the crushed seed into the forest, but his shoulders remained stiff, watchful.

"Foolish wolf," Elin said. "Someone else might well have wanted the power you so lightly cast aside."

Matthew looked at me, a question in his eyes.

I didn't know how to answer it. Part of me longed to make him gather the pieces of crushed seed up again, in hopes that some power might remain in them. "You have no protection now."

I heard his breath speed up, saw the small pulse that pounded in the side of his neck. He was still afraid, afraid of me. I smelled his fear, a sharp tang in the humid air. Had the faerie folk always smelled my fear, too?

"I understand why you and Allie ate the seeds." Matthew's voice was the one steady thing about him. "I know too well what glamour is like, and why you want to be safe from it."

He knew it better than me. The Lady had held him under glamour for so long. "Then why—"

"Because I don't want to use glamour on anyone else, not now, not ever."

I flinched at his quiet words. "I'm—" But I couldn't say I was sorry, because I wasn't sure I was.

"You wouldn't have to use it." Allie twisted a lock of hair around her fingers, and I knew she felt as uneasy as me. "I don't plan to."

Matthew looked at Elin. "I don't know about anyone else, but I *know* I'm not better than you." He pulled his shirt back on. "I know the things I'd do if I had this power. That's why I can't take it."

I wanted to be sorry—that wasn't enough. I wanted to pull him close, so close that I could pretend everything was all right. I reached for him. He reached for me, and something sleepy crept back into his eyes.

I drew a sharp breath. Was that sleepiness only him wanting to hold me in turn, or was it something more? How could I ever know if his wants were truly the same as mine, or whether I just wished them to be?

I jerked my arms back to my sides. I couldn't know, and that meant I had to set my own wanting aside. "I don't want to hurt you." I'd sooner draw my own blood than his.

"I know," Matthew said, his eyes clear once more. But he didn't reach for me again.

"Caleb and Karin never used it." Allie stuck out her lower lip. "We can learn not to use it, too."

"You think glamour can be turned off at will, as easily as hooding a hawk sends it to sleep? I do not know how much practice it took for my mother and uncle to cease using glamour so completely. I only know they used it freely enough when I was young." No laughter in Elin's words now. "Let me go, Liza. Entertaining though this may be, we have work to do beyond the Arch."

"*Be free,*" I said, releasing my magic's hold on her. Then, "Why didn't you say someone still followed us?"

"As I recall, we had a few more pressing concerns."

Elin moved to put a hand to the Arch's surface. "Now, I cannot speak for the rest of you, but I intend to do all I can for my mother." She stepped into the metal and was gone.

Right. First we'd save Karin, or fail to save her. Everything else would come after. I walked to the Arch as well. Allie grabbed my stone hand. I reached for Matthew with my good one. His steps were so much louder than Allie's and mine.

He hesitated, just for an instant. As his fingers closed around mine, I saw the apology in his gray eyes.

"Maybe you should stay behind." My whisper sounded loud in the night. "I'm not the only one you'll have to worry about in Faerie." It was much more dangerous for him to go there than me now.

Matthew shook his head, no doubt in that gesture. "I came this far to find you. I'm not leaving you now."

"All right." We'd deal with this later, too—somehow. I looked into the Arch. *Faerie. Show me Faerie.*

The visions were reluctant to come, like fire to wet wood. It took a long time before I saw—

Karin, rocking back and forth as she crooned to what remained of the First Tree, while in the near distance, other dead tree stumps crumbled to dust—

Nys, standing in a stone cavern set with gems of all colors, faerie folk gathered around him. At the room's center was another standing stone. He walked through it, and the others followed, holding to one another as surely as Allie and Matthew and I did—

"Liza." Matthew's low hiss drew me out of the vision. I blinked my eyes open in time to see Nys stepping out of the Arch, all of Faerie behind him.

⌒ *Chapter 17* ⌒

Faerie folk poured from both legs of the Arch, the one we stood by and the farther one, too. So many—Nys couldn't be the only seer leading them. As they gathered at the center of the stone platform, Matthew, Allie, and I backed away. What would happen to my world with so many faerie folk in it? Elin and the Lady alone had destroyed entire towns.

I shivered in the chill air. This was more than three humans could handle, with protection from glamour or without it. I put myself between the fey and Allie and Matthew, but they returned to my sides as Nys's gaze fell on us.

"So you return to witness our final exile, humans?" There was dust on Nys's hands and scarred face. "I do not know how you escaped, but I cannot believe you are here out of concern for our well-being or to mourn the ending of the Realm. Even so, we might make some use of you yet." His eyes narrowed, like a hawk honing in on prey. "Allie. Come here."

Anger flared in me. After all that had happened, he still saw Allie as just a tool to be used for as long as possible, until like all tools she wore out.

But Allie was no more fully human than I was now. Her hold on my wrist remained firm. "You can't take me over, not anymore," she said.

Nys frowned. "Given more time, I would have the truth of how it is you and Liza have both slipped my control. As it is, there are other ways of gaining your cooperation." He bent to touch the platform, and its stone grabbed hold of my feet and Matthew's boots. I tried to wrench free, but the rock swiftly flowed past our knees.

I reached with my good hand to push it away, and stone grasped my fingers. I snatched them back, feeling pinpricks of rock in my skin. I drew my other hand close as other faerie folk moved to surround us.

"Now, Healer," Nys said. "If you don't wish me to command this stone to rise farther and squeeze the very air and life from them, you will come with me."

"You could just *ask*." Anger burned in Allie's words.

Beside me, I heard the pounding of Matthew's heart as he gauged the crowd. Maybe he could shift his way free—his wolf's legs were thinner than his human ones—but what then? The faerie folk had stopped exiting the Arch. There were a couple hundred of them, many with bags slung over their shoulders or backs, some with hooded hawks or wakeful owls on their arms. A few of the fey, clearly ill, were carried by others. I did not see Tolven—the only one who might not wish us dead—among them. As a wolf, Matthew could attack Nys, but there were too many who'd attack Matthew in turn. I had Nys's name, but I didn't have anyone else's.

That meant we had to talk our way free. "*Nys,*" I said.

Nys looked down at me. "I have already told you that is not my true name."

"No." My voice was hard as the stone that now moved up my thighs. "But I do know your true name. And if you do not release us, I will use it."

"Human lies," Nys spat. "Of the few here who know my name, none would share it with you."

"Kaylen would." A few of the fey exchanged glances. Most of them didn't know Caleb had survived the War. "Shall I speak the name he gave me to everyone here? Or will you let us go? We do not seek to harm you. We only seek to pass through the Arch."

"And where is my son," Nys said coldly, "that you have so recently been in his confidence?"

Allie made a strangled sound. Matthew's fingers found mine, and that small comfort made me want to cry.

"He's gone." I forced the words out into the night, where nothing could take them back. "He died saving his student."

"His human student?" Nys asked, his voice deadly soft.

"Yes," I said. "You pushed too hard when you made her heal." Nys hadn't made Allie kill the owl, though. He hadn't made me bring Allie back. Yet this would never have begun if not for him.

"My son has long been a fool. He has long paid prices higher than any of us could afford." Nys's voice remained quiet. He gave Allie an appraising look. "I hope you intend to be worthy of this sacrifice, Healer."

Allie lifted her head. "That's exactly what I intend."

"Let us go," I said, "and I will hold your name safe. Make any move to harm us, and I'll speak it so that all here may know it." There were enough fey to make up a large town, if there were a town with no children in it. Surely Nys had enemies enough among them.

Nys touched the stone platform, and it released Matthew and me. "I give you your lives." His eyes lingered on Allie, as if she were a pet he was reluctant to set free. "Nothing more. You will come with us, all of you." Around us, the silent fey waited, as if on Nys's word.

He wasn't their ruler. Faerie wasn't run by a Council like my town was. "If you let us go," I said, "I will do what I can to return Karinna to you. That's what you and Elin wanted when you stole me away, isn't it?" I wasn't sure Karin wanted to be returned to her people—or that I wanted her to be—but we'd figure that out later. First we had to save her.

A whisper of breath rippled through the gathered fey. They didn't know Karin lived, either.

"We have survived without Karinna the Fierce for some time. We will survive a time longer, until this world, like ours, falls to dust. If you wish your freedom, you shall have to offer better than that."

"Fine! *I'll* offer you something." Allie shoved her hair out of her face and looked right up at Nys. "After we save Karin, I'll go with you and keep healing your people, even though you can't make me do it anymore."

"No!" I grabbed Allie's hand. She pulled it away.

"It's not up to you, Liza." Allie kept looking at Nys. "But I get to demand some things, too. Like that I won't stay with you all the time, because I also have my own town to take care of. And that you promise to protect me if any of the fey try to hurt me, because I can't heal anyone if I'm dead."

Nys regarded her with a cool stare, as if Allie weren't offering him far more than he deserved. He deserved to die himself after all he'd done. "And why should I trust you to serve us, Healer, after I have used you ill?"

"I'm not serving you. I'm doing what's right. Just like I keep telling you. Caleb would do the same, you know." Allie bit her lip. "I hate what happened so much. If it were up to me, I'd undo it all. But I can't, so I'm going to make it worth something. I'll be more careful this time. It's easier to be careful when you're not afraid. I'll try not to push too hard—you also have to promise not to make me push too hard. But I'll take the chance."

Nys looked to the dark sky. "You would truly come with us? Leave your people to walk among so many of mine, after all the harm you did to us during the War?"

"Careful," Matthew whispered.

"And after all the harm you did to us, too," Allie said. "Yes."

"We do not need the help of humans," a woman said. I recognized her: the woman who had guarded the sickroom.

"This is true enough for you and I," Nys said, looking back to Allie. "Yet I will accept the healer's offer, not for my own sake, but for that of our people." He bowed to Allie, as respectfully as Tolven had bowed to me. "I agree to your conditions, Healer." Nys stepped aside, leaving a clear path to the Arch. "Do what you must, and then see that you keep your word and return to me, or it will reflect badly on all your people."

I grabbed Allie's hand again, and this time I didn't let go. I had no idea how I would keep her safe from Nys now.

I looked to Matthew. He hunched his shoulders. "I don't like it, either," he whispered. "But Allie's right—it's not up to us." He laid his hand on my other arm as I walked back to the Arch.

"Your trust in us is charming, Liza," Nys said. "But it is not you with whom I have exchanged vows this day."

A whisper of wind brushed the Arch, echoing off of something hollow inside. Nys had given me little reason to trust him. I looked into the Arch's surface. *Show me Faerie.* Light came to it slower still, but then I saw—

Tolven, in an underground cavern surrounded by dying brown plants, his quia seed in hand. "I want to keep you," he whispered to it. "But you do not want to be kept. And this has never been only about me." He drew a breath and called, "Grow!" The seed's shell cracked, and a bright green shoot began to unfurl—

Gray dust, casting haze into the air, and around the haze the empty dark, moving closer, ever closer. Through the haze, I saw a few burned trees, and the standing stone, and Elin, approaching her mother, trying to catch hold of the hem of Karin's shirt. Karin whirled around, aiming a kick at Elin's legs, and Elin toppled into the dust. She scrambled to her feet, eyeing Karin, looking for another chance to approach—

In the distance, I heard footsteps—our watcher, moving closer again. Nys would have to deal with that. I stepped into the dust. Stone pressed close around me, pressing the air from my chest—and then I was free, gulping air once more, air that held the scent of dying rooms, cut off from light and air and hope, for all that we stood beneath the night sky. I coughed as I looked around.

We stood beside the standing stone, in an island of faint color: gray stumps, black sky, white stars, Elin and Karin in their shades of green and brown. Karin crouched by the First Tree, humming to it as if it were a child, but brown shoots no longer grew at her command. From her pocket, I felt a hint of green life from the seed she carried.

Elin knelt by her mother's side, despair clear enough in the set of her shoulders. A few dozen yards away in any direction, dust hung heavy in the air, and beyond the dust lay the cold darkness of the crumbling. That darkness was shot through with faint strands of silver, just as it had been at the crossroads. I heard as well as saw them, a faint thrumming in the air, near the edge of hearing.

"This is bad," Allie whispered as she and Matthew dropped my hands.

Elin stood at our approach. "I see you have deigned to join me at last." She limped slightly, and a purple bruise had flowered on her cheek. Karin was not easy to rescue.

"Ran into some faerie folk." Matthew wrapped his arms around himself as he took in the bleak land around us. The air remained warm, but the wind that whispered through it was cold and stale.

Elin glanced at her mother. "How many?"

An uneasy laugh escaped Matthew's lips. "All of them, I think."

"That is some small comfort, then," Elin said. "For it means my people have escaped this crumbling for a short time more, until the human world, too, falls to dust."

It would be no comfort to the humans subject to faerie glamour. "This isn't right," I said. "We weren't away for long enough for so much to crumble away."

"Do you not know how things unravel?" Elin rubbed at her arms. I wondered if more bruises lay beneath her cloak. "First there is a snag, then a small run in the fabric. It can stay like that a long time. For all the years since the War. But once a weaving comes undone, once something pulls the snagged thread, it goes quickly, the weight of all that time behind it. And so Rhianne's long watch over Mirinda and all her children fails at last."

"The War," I said. "That was the snag."

"No doubt," Elin said. "The War was when the crumbling began. The fires your people sent were strong indeed. But I do not know what pulled the thread."

It wasn't the fires alone that had caused the crumbling. I knew that now. It was the death Rhianne's roots kept away from her people and the effect of the War's many dead flooding the gray those roots held. I looked to the First Tree and saw Rhianne's shadow arms stretching toward the sky. Had Mirinda known the price of her mother's gifts before she'd passed from the Realm? But that would have been countless years before the War, and the only prices paid then were paid by humans.

I circled the tree, looking for some way to touch Karin. I reached for her wrist. Karin hissed, a sound like rain on hot stone, and I drew back.

"We need a distraction," Matthew said. "So Allie can get closer. Maybe if we all approach at once . . ."

Distract me from my work here no longer, Rhianne had said, *lest you hasten that which you seek to prevent.* I remembered a flash of green, the very fabric of the gray gone slack as I tried to wrench the summoner free of it, until she seized control once more.

The wind cut through my sweater, raising bumps on my skin. The War was the snag, yes. But the War wasn't what had pulled on the thread once the snag had caught.

I was.

When my people make a mistake, we try to set things right. Elin's words, but I'd always believed it, too. It wouldn't have been a mistake if Rhianne hadn't taken control again. But she had, and so instead of fixing things, I'd made them far worse.

How could a mistake this large be mine?

It didn't matter how. I had to set it right. I looked up at the First Tree's shadow branches—Rhianne's arms, grasping at the sky, at more than anyone should hold. I craned my neck and saw what might have been shadow leaves or might have been flowing hair. No doubt Rhianne had only sought to set things right, too.

I'd tried to push her out of the gray from within it and failed. What if I pulled her to me from outside of the gray instead?

"I think I can provide a distraction," I said. One that Karin, focused on the First Tree as she was, would surely notice. "Ready, Allie?"

"You know I am," Allie said.

Elin gave me a level look. "Care to tell us what you intend? Or do you prefer to play a guessing game?"

I looked right back at her. "I intend to call Rhianne," I said.

~ *Chapter 18* ~

"**Y**ou cannot be serious," Elin said. "You cannot expect Rhianne will answer a human call when she has spoken with none of her own people since the War and has never spoken with any but plant speakers regardless."

"Who's Rhianne?" Matthew asked.

"A summoner. And she already has spoken to me."

"*The* summoner," Elin said. "The first of our people. One does not trouble her lightly."

The wind was growing colder. I drew breath to call.

Before I could, the ground lurched beneath us. Stone shattered, and a tree—not the First Tree, a new tree—burst through the cracks, a tree with cinnamon-brown bark whose perfect green leaves unfurled as they grew, green so bright it burned my eyes. A quia tree. The life in it pulled on me, as familiar as the life in the seeds I'd once held, but I hadn't called this new tree, which held nothing of Rhianne within it. Karin's crooning fell silent.

"Mother?" Elin said.

The plant speaker crouched into a protective stance, as if the new tree were one more threat she faced. Her magic hadn't called it, either, as far as I could tell; I still felt the pull of the untouched quia seed in her pocket. *Tolven,* I thought, remembering my vision. Tolven had a quia seed, too.

Karin opened her mouth to speak, but the sounds that came out were tree sounds: branches creaking in the wind, roots moaning as they soaked up rain. She stood and stalked toward the new tree.

Allie darted forward. There was a flash of silver light, and Karin crumpled gracelessly to the ground. Allie knelt to run her hands over Karin's body. "She's all right. I mean, her body's all right. I don't know about the rest."

Elin let out a breath. "Let us take her from this place, then."

Elin and Matthew lifted Karin together. They stepped through the standing stone, and I took Allie's hand to follow.

It trembled in mine, as if Allie were the one who'd been stunned. "I *hate* this," she said. "This isn't what healing is *for.*"

I knew it wasn't just Karin she meant. "You didn't have to kill the owl. You could have let me go."

"You could have let *me* go." Allie sighed. "And Caleb could have let me go, too. It's so hard, isn't it? Deciding what to do. Caleb was better at it. I'm still learning, you know?"

"I know. I'm learning, too." I looked into the stone. *The Arch*, I thought. *Show me the Arch.*

The light that came to the stone was sluggish as muddy water. We waited several long heartbeats until I saw—

A woman running toward the Arch, a woman I'd seen in visions before, her long clear braid flowing behind her. The Arch let her pass through its surface as readily as the forest had let her through its brambles. She disappeared from view, and instead I saw—

Matthew and Elin setting Karin down beside the Arch, while Nys frowned as he watched them—

I stepped toward that vision, back into my own world. The air grew sticky with moisture. The stale smell of Faerie faded but didn't go away.

Allie ran to Karin, pressing hands to her chest. Matthew straightened Karin's arms by her sides. He, Elin, and Nys were the only others here. The sky was as dark in my world as in Faerie, but seeing in the dark wasn't a problem for me, not anymore. I heard the soft breathing of the rest of the fey from where they waited deeper in the forest, clustered in small groups, as if they couldn't find any larger space free of the crumbling. If our follower also watched us, I couldn't tell beneath the sound of so many.

"I thought it best not to have a crowd when Karinna returned," Nys said dryly. "Someone might try to stop her when she abandons us again."

"She won't abandon us," Elin said. "Not this time. No matter what you might hope, Nys."

"I helped you bring her back," Nys said. "I serve our people, Elin, always. Remember that. I was not the one who was absent when the time came to lead them from the Realm at last."

"Stop it, both of you!" Light bloomed beneath Allie's hands, gentle silver light that flowed over Karin and bathed all of us in its glow.

The light faded, leaving us surrounded by night once more. Karin didn't move.

"What is wrong?" Elin demanded.

"Nothing." Allie's voice was a thread near to snapping. "She's awake. She should be fine, but—"

The River murmured between its banks. "I could try calling her," I said, uncertain.

"There is no need for that." Karin sat up with a deliberateness that said her silence had been a choice.

Her voice was steady, sane. I grabbed her hand, and she squeezed it. Elin's voice caught on a sob. I looked at the weaver, and she smiled, really smiled. I smiled back, daring for the first time to believe Karin would truly be all right.

"I gather I have been gone some time." Karin spoke with as much care as she'd moved. She opened her eyes, though they did not focus. "I would know where I am, and who is here with me. I hear Elin, Liza, Allie. There are two others. There are many others, but only two close by."

"Matthew." He was smiling, too. "And we're at the Arch."

"Nys." He didn't smile. "It is good to see you, Karinna."

"If that is so, it is no doubt for reasons of your own." Karin gave a dry chuckle. "And, Matthew, there is a story in your being here. But first: Elin, Nys, have you harmed the others in any way?"

The smile drained from Elin's face. "Even now, at the Realm's own ending, humans matter to you more than your own people?"

Karin's expression went steel hard. "No, Daughter. They do not matter more. But neither do they matter less. And you have not answered my question."

"We're fine now," I said.

"I risked my own life and left my own people to look after your precious humans." Elin's voice was just as hard. "Does that please you?"

Karin rested her head on one hand. "Elin."

"You need not worry about me," Elin said. "Unlike you, I plan to return home. There is only one person left in the Realm now who can call a quia tree to grow, though I know not how a seed came into his keeping. I'll not abandon him, though the land itself crumble away. Indeed, Nys, I'll not soon forget that you left Toby behind."

"Staying was the plant speaker's choice, not mine," Nys said. "If he could not be persuaded to follow us, it was not for lack of trying."

Elin ignored him. She gave her mother a stiff bow, though Karin could not see it. "I am glad you are well, Mother, and I am sorry for any harm I have caused you." She stepped through the Arch at that and was gone.

Karin pressed her fingers against her forehead. "It is difficult to speak with you, Daughter, if you persist in running away." She stood, and Allie darted to her side to steady her. Karin felt her way to the Arch, Allie guiding her once she saw where she was heading. Karin ran a hand along the smooth metal. "The crumbling smells strong here. It was not nearly so strong on the path between our towns."

"It might be worse there, too, by now." I felt a shiver of fear for Mom, and the baby, and all my town. "Karin, I have to go back to Faerie, too." I still had to call—to try to call—Rhianne out of the gray.

Matthew's brows drew together. He rubbed the scar at his wrist. "Why, Liza?"

"Yes, why?" Nys asked. "What could possibly be left in our dying world for you? No matter—I have pledged to grant you your freedom, and if you wish to throw your life away with it, that is no concern of mine. I have my own people to see to, and Allie has a promise to keep."

"Careful, stone shaper," Karin said. "They are my people, not yours, by oaths you yourself have taken." Did Nys pale a little? Karin knelt to trace a crack in the stone. "What promise, Allie?"

Allie knelt beside her. "I'm going with Nys. To help heal the Faerie folk. I gave him my word."

A small green shoot broke through the stone. Karin stroked it gently. She wouldn't let Allie go with Nys. Of course she wouldn't.

"It's the right thing to do, Karin." Allie ran a hand through her hair, making it stand on end. "If you'd seen how sick they were in Faerie, you'd say so, too. It's like when you and Caleb came to our town, and we didn't deserve your help but you gave it to us anyway."

Karin laced her fingers together, letting the green go. "And no doubt my people would not accept my brother as healer in your place, even were he willing to return to them."

Silence then, save for the distant breathing of the faerie folk and the chirping of an early sparrow.

The green shoot wilted and fell. Karin did not move. "Tell me," she said.

"It was my fault." My throat ached with every word. "He died fixing my mistake—one of my mistakes." My knees shook. Matthew steadied me. I saw no blame in his gray eyes, not for this.

Karin stood and turned toward the Arch. "So, Youngest Brother. It is you who finds escape after all." For a heartbeat she leaned her head against the metal, as if for support. Then she turned back to us. "Allie. Liza. Matthew. Every teacher knows the risk they take when they accept students. Later, when we have time, I will want to hear all that has happened. Until then, know this: Caleb and I both chose the sacrifices we would make long ago, as humans measure time, and we vowed there would be no regrets. We agreed to pay the prices we needed to pay to save the things we could save."

Matthew leaned on me, too, as if it were all we could do to keep each other standing. "I'd change it all if I could," I said.

"I know." There was no blame in Karin's words, either. "Allie. Come here." Karin reached out her hands, but Allie threw herself around her with a sob.

Karin held her close. "Nys has, I assume, offered you promises of protection?"

"He has indeed," Nys said. "You need not worry on that account. Your pet humans have negotiated well. The healer will be safe."

"Not safe enough, if it is pets you see them as still. But you will treat her well. I will see to it, for I intend to travel with you, for a time at least."

I let out a breath. If Karin was with Allie, she'd be as safe as she possibly could be.

"You did not deem remaining with your people necessary after the War," Nys said. "What has changed, that Karinna the Fierce worries about us now?"

"I do not believe I am obligated to share my reasons with you, any more than you are free to disobey my wishes. I am yet heir to the Realm, and here, where my mind is my own, you have much to answer for." Karin put her hands on Allie's shoulders. Allie looked up at her, eyes glistening. "You do your teacher honor," Karin said.

Allie swallowed. "I'm trying to." She walked over to solemnly hug first Matthew, then me.

"I'm—" But I still couldn't say it. "I'm not sorry I

saved you. I'm sorry for what happened because of it, but I'm not sorry for that."

"I know. I—" Allie shook her head. "I'll see you soon, okay? Promise?"

I didn't know what would happen when I went back to Faerie, when I tried to call Rhianne. "If I can. Promise."

Allie brushed a hand across her eyes and walked to Nys's side. "Okay. Let's go."

"Wait for me with the rest of our people," Karin told him. "I must speak with Liza and Matthew. Give us"—she tilted her head—"until the first light of dawn, if the crumbling allows it. Return for me then."

Nys bowed his head. "As you wish, my liege." He spoke the last word as if it tasted bad. He took Allie's hand, and together they disappeared into the forest. I heard Nys's steps, a whisper of movement against the damp earth, and Allie's, no louder. Karin turned back to us as their steps faded. "Now, quickly. Tell me why you must return to the Realm, Liza."

"And me." Matthew sat cross-legged on the ground, and I sat beside him. Karin sat, too. I told them both, as quickly as I could, about Rhianne, and the crumbling, and how I had made the crumbling worse. More dawn birds joined the sparrow as I spoke, though the sky remained dark.

"So you see," I said. "This is mine to fix, or die failing

to fix." Matthew gave me a sharp look, but I pressed on. "I need to do everything I possibly can to call Rhianne out of the gray. To stop the crumbling before everything is lost."

"The price of my people's gifts." Pain flashed like lightning in Karin's eyes. "I did not know it was so high. I have learned, since the War, how much your people have suffered for those gifts, but I did not know all of it. This mistake did not begin with you, Liza. You are only one small part of something that started long before you were born."

"But if I can do something about it—I already failed once, and that made things so much worse—I have to keep trying, don't I?" This was too important not to.

"You are strong," Karin said. "We both know this. Rhianne is stronger, strong enough that her tree survived the burning of my land when so much else was lost. I heard that land all too well, with my mother gone, where before I only heard the plants and their dying. That's the reason my mind so swiftly slid from my grasp. I don't remember much of what happened in the Realm. But I remember too well how deeply the land was injured and how much pain it yet feels. That the First Tree stands at all, damaged though it is, tells me that uprooting Rhianne will be no small task. And I fear

Rhianne will do all she can to destroy you, should you fail."

A gray strip of sky was dawning across the River. Matthew's arm pressed against mine, but I could not feel his fingers around my stone hand. I leaned against him, hoping it wasn't my wanting making him draw near, because I needed him here so badly. I didn't know if I could make Rhianne hear me, but I knew that if I did, and failed, I wasn't likely to survive to try again. "But can it be done?" I pressed.

"I do not know. Perhaps. It is not impossible. But it is such a small chance." More green shoots sprouted along the crack in the stone. Karin ran her fingers through them. "It is not right, that you pay the price for what my people have done. You do not deserve that."

Almost, I believed her. "But none of us deserve all the things that happen to us, do we?" Both the good and the bad—we were better and worse than it all. "No one deserved the War," I said.

"Just so." Karin reached into her pocket and held something out: the last quia seed. "Take it," she said, and I did. "Perhaps this will be more help to you than it was to me. The seeds were always meant for you. But I would stand beside you if I could."

"You can't. Not in Faerie." I slid the seed into my

pocket. There was no knowing how long Karin's mind would stay her own if she went back.

"No, I can't," Karin said. "And not only because madness would render me useless. I do not know how long your world will resist the crumbling after mine falls to it, but however long that may be, I cannot allow so many of my people to enter your world together, free to use their power as they will. I must have oaths from them—not to use glamour and not to harm your people with their other magics—before I let them go any farther."

"But I can go with Liza." Matthew turned to me. "I am going. You know that, don't you?"

"No." I drew my hand from his. He wasn't a summoner. He couldn't do anything against Rhianne, and if I fell, he'd have no way of leaving Faerie on his own. If I didn't return, I needed to know that Matthew, at least, would be safe, for as long as this world held. "There's nothing you can do, not this time. Go with Karin and Allie, Matthew. Please."

Matthew was silent, as if thinking about that. At last he said quietly, "All right."

I wrapped my arms around him, wanting to remember the feel of holding him, the scent of his hair and his skin and his sweat—everything. "Someone needs to go home," I said. "To Mom and the others. To tell them what's happened."

"All right," Matthew said again, his voice just the same: flat, expressionless. I saw the sleepy emptiness in his face, and I knew. This decision was not his own.

Karin raised her head. "Liza," she said softly. "What are you doing?"

"Keeping him safe." Shame heated my face—what was shame beside Matthew's life? If I was going to sacrifice myself, I could at least save him, and he could hate me all he wanted afterward. I'd be gone.

"I see," Karin said. She could hate me for this, too. It didn't matter. I didn't want anyone else dying for me.

Karin stood, and the green sprouts retreated beneath the stone. "You are changed, Liza. Allie, as well. I sensed it when I woke, but I believed it a matter that could wait. I was wrong. Are you aware that there is a part of me that wants nothing so dearly as to forbid you to return to my world? That even as we speak, that part would have you go back to your town, to live under whatever protection it can provide, for as long as it might hold?"

"I know that." I stood, too, wishing, like Karin wished, that there was a better way.

"No. I do not think you do." A dangerous edge crept into Karin's voice. "Because if I wished to, I could stop you. Blind though I am, I have battle skill enough remaining to render you unable to walk. I could send you home with Nys and Allie and Matthew, and you could not stop me. Shall I show you?"

There was no warning. Her leg swept forward, and mine buckled beneath me. I crashed into the stone, and Karin's knee jabbed my stomach, throwing me onto my back, while Matthew watched through sleepy eyes. I threw my hands over my head, waiting for the next blow. I'd never feared Karin before.

The blow didn't come. Karin stood and turned from me. I curled into a crouch, protecting my bruised stomach.

Karin looked toward the Arch, as if she could see something in its surface. "Humans have always been so fragile, so easily broken. I have always been more powerful than any of the humans I taught. But I have not used that power against them, not since the War ended. Kaylen is—was—not as powerful as me, but he had power enough, and he did the same. I do not know for certain how my people's gifts have come to you, Liza, though I have some ideas. But I know well the temptations of power and the desire to use it against others for their own good. So now you know it, too. What will you do?"

Matthew blinked, as if only mildly puzzled by what he saw. "Shall I go now?" he asked. He would do anything I wanted. Anything.

"No." The word came out low, and hoarse, and it

made my chest ache. I wanted so badly to keep him safe. "No, Matthew." I let him go, feeling something fall slack between us as I stood. "It's not up to me."

Matthew shuddered back into himself, eyes focusing, breath speeding up. I smelled fear on him once more, and I turned away, ashamed. At the horizon, dawn was growing, streaking the sky pink, but the birds had fallen silent.

"Fragile things are precious, Liza." Karin's voice sounded very far away. "Never forget that. You can break a thing by holding it too close as easily as by casting it aside."

"Well, I'll try not to be *too* fragile." Matthew laughed uneasily as he stood. I felt his arms wrap around me, and I knew this was one more thing I didn't deserve. "I won't leave you, Liza, not if I have a choice. Not like the last time you faced powerful magic. Maybe there's something I can do. If not, at least I can watch. You need a watcher, someone focused on something other than the magic. I don't want to survive this knowing I left you alone."

I trembled in his hold. "I wish you would go." It was all I could do to keep the glamour from my voice.

"I know you do," Matthew said.

The murmuring River fell as silent as the birds had. I looked to the horizon, but the dawn light was gone, replaced by the darkness of the crumbling, rolling over the water like black storm clouds shot through with faint silver threads. Karin made a low sound.

Allie came running through the forest. "Nys says we need to leave now."

"Yes." Karin stumbled, and Matthew pulled away to catch her. "The River—something's tearing, letting the Realm and its crumbling through. I can hear the land—my dying land—I cannot stay here." Karin reached for me, and I grabbed her hand. She drew me into a swift, fierce hug. "You do your teacher honor, too. Never doubt it. If we do not meet again here, perhaps we'll meet beyond the gray. If you see Elianna—" She shook her head, dismissing whatever she'd meant to say.

Allie took her arm. The healer gave us both a thin smile, and then she and Karin headed into the forest.

Matthew took my hand, his fingers brushing the sensitive place where stone met skin. "Ready?" he asked, and some part of me was glad he would be with me after all. I smelled his fear still, but he reached out and took my face in his hands. "Just so you know," he whispered. "This is me." His eyes clear and focused, he leaned down and pressed his lips against mine. I pressed mine back, inhaling wolf and sweat and boy and, beneath it all, the staleness of the crumbling, growing stronger. I pulled away, knowing we had little time.

"Later," Matthew whispered, like a promise: that there would be a later, and that in it, we would find a way to cope with glamour, just like we'd find a way to cope with everything else. I wasn't sure I believed those things, so I let him believe for me, just as once I'd believed in spring for him. Holding his hand once more, I looked into the Arch.

Show me Faerie. It took several heartbeats, but at last I saw—

Elin, pulling a struggling Tolven away from roots he clung to like a stubborn child and dragging him down a tunnel whose glowing stones flickered out, one by one—

Dust. Endless gray dust, turning standing stone and tree stumps to shadow—

I stepped into that dust, Matthew at my side.

～ *Chapter 19* ～

I choked on the smell of dry, musty air. Cold air, so much colder than before. Elin and Tolven stared at us, breathing hard, gray ash dusting their shoulders and hair. It clearly hadn't been easy for Elin to drag Tolven to the surface. Dust was everywhere, a gray haze that blocked the thin morning light. That light ended after only a couple dozen paces in any direction, giving way to icy darkness.

Rhianne's tree remained, a few yards away, but the other stumps were gone, save for Tolven's full-grown quia tree, whose bright green leaves cast the only true color here. Faint silver threads shone through the dark around us, casting an eerie glow over the air, as if Faerie itself were a magic that someone was trying to work.

Elin laughed. "Trust Liza to show up in time for the end of the world. Too bad we can't join you, but we were just leaving."

"Not leaving!" Tolven screeched. He ran sharp nails along his sleeves, but they couldn't pierce the fabric. "The tree is green. I stay with the tree."

Elin grabbed his arm. "You cannot stay here. No one can stay here."

"*She* can." Tolven tilted his head at me. "You carry green, too." Something in his gaze slid into focus. He reached for the seed in my pocket, stopped himself. "Liza, yes?"

"Yes," I said.

"It is good to see you again." Tolven bowed respectfully. "You know, don't you? That this is not over yet. I need to stay with the tree, to make sure it doesn't die. The tree is needed. Tell Elin. She doesn't understand."

Elin's grip tightened around Tolven's wrist. "What I don't understand," she said softly, "is how your words are suddenly clear."

Tolven gave her a sweet, sad smile. "I fear it will not last. I fear all the green will be needed, by the end."

I looked to Tolven's quia tree. It had distracted Karin, letting us get her free, but if it had any power to stop the crumbling, I didn't know of it.

There was so little of Faerie left. If I failed this time, surely there would be no escaping its ending. "You don't want to stay here, Toby. Not for this."

"The tree says to stay." Tolven sounded very sure.

Something stiffened about Elin's jaw. I realized she would no more leave Tolven than Matthew would leave me, and that there was a reason Tolven had asked for her when we'd first met. I knew less about Elin and her life here than I thought.

I couldn't make their decisions for them, any more than I could anyone else's. With Matthew's hand wrapped around mine, I walked to Rhianne's tree.

"You take care of the magic," Matthew said. "I'll stand watch over the rest."

I wanted to draw him to me again, but if I did, I might send him away after all. I released his hand to stand before the tree.

"We shall all keep watch," Elin said. "Over whatever scheme it is that has brought you back here. After all, if the rest of you are to stay, I cannot have it said that I alone lack courage."

"Your mother wants—" Karin hadn't said what she wanted, but I could guess easily enough. "She wants you to return to her, if you can."

Elin brushed her hands over her cloak, making it

shimmer. "It has been a long time since my mother dictated my actions."

I swallowed, tasting staleness at the back of my throat. Karin had saved me, but she hadn't saved Elin. "It's much the same with my mother," I said. Mom, who had saved the other Afters but not me, and who I wanted to get home to just the same.

Elin bowed her head. "I am sorry for that."

I was sorry, too, but there was nothing I could do to change it. What I could do was lift my head to the shadow branches that rose from the First Tree's stump.

"Rhianne!" I threw all my strength, all my magic, into that call. *"Come here, Rhianne!"* The air grew colder. My breath came out in frosty puffs. Branches creaked far above, like a tree in an ice storm.

A voice inside me whispered, *"Liza. Come here."* Rhianne's voice, a low hiss that shuddered through my bones. My shadow slid from my body, as easily as a bean from its pod.

"Liza!" Matthew caught my body as it toppled, but his call held no magic.

"Come." It was Rhianne's call that pulled my shadow slowly and surely toward the tree, into the tree. The threads of the world flared bright around me, and in that brightness I saw—

*A faerie woman with a long twisting braid, kneeling
before the First Tree, a silver quia leaf hanging from her
neck. "You will speak with me now, Mother." A stone
knife flashed in the air. "We will speak indeed—"*

Brightness and visions drained away like a bad dream,
leaving me standing on a gray featureless plain. Before
me, shadows swirled around the First Tree's roots, roots
taller than I was. Beside me, green life whispered from
the quia seed Karin had given me. Farther away, I saw
a second tree, but otherwise there was nothing but gray
shadow.

Liza, I thought. *I am Liza.* I would not know it if not
for the seed. Cold filled me, the cold and the darkness
that lay at the heart of us all.

I looked to the First Tree's roots and the hollows
among them, which swirled with the shadows of the
dead. I would have to push the summoner away after
all. *"Go, Rhianne!"*

*"Stop, Liza! There will be no more of your summon-
ing here!"* Rhianne's words snapped like breaking wood,
her voice both within me and without, now that I stood
in the gray. My own words froze in my throat. I moved
my lips, trying to force my magic free, but I couldn't. My
chest tightened, and my vision swam, though I shouldn't
need air, not here. I was bound, as surely as when Nys

had pressed my hand to the stone. Just like that, I had failed after all.

I stopped trying to use my magic, and my body—my shadow—relaxed, though I still felt Rhianne's magic around me like an icy, shimmering net. I hadn't failed with Nys in the end. I remained alert for anything I could do, as surely as I had in a stone room with no visible way out.

"That's better. I grow weary of you and your power, Liza. Now, let go the seed you carry." Rhianne's words weren't a command, not yet. "You may do it of your own will, or else I will do all I can to compel you. The time for kindness is past. You will endanger my people no longer."

"Your people flee the results of your protection." Without magic in them, the words left my lips easily enough. "Faerie crumbles away."

"You say this, yet my people live, those the burning and other misfortune did not take. I'll not believe the world gone while my people remain."

"They won't remain long," I said. "Your people flee from Faerie into my world, but the crumbling moves to my world as well. Nowhere is safe so long as you keep holding on to the gray. This has to end. Nothing lasts forever." As soon as I said it, I felt the truth of it.

Nothing, faerie or human, could hold for all time. Cities fell. Stones crumbled. Plants gave way to mold and dirt. People fell, and the roots of trees ate them and grew strong. The world had always been winding down, even Before.

Why save anything, then? I thought of all I'd left behind in my world, all those I cared for, every forest path I'd walked, every field I'd tilled, and I found I wanted to save them all the more fiercely knowing they would die. Besides, things grew from mold and from dirt, too.

Fragile things are precious, Liza. "Your people are dying, Rhianne, just like mine. Let them go, before both our worlds crumble away." I thought of Allie, pulling on my hand before this very tree, begging *me* to let go. I hadn't listened, either.

"You lie, Summoner, though I do not know how. Until my daughter walks here, I'll not believe the world is gone."

"Will you believe it now, then?" A woman's arch voice, rich as velvet. I turned to see a shadow striding toward us, a shadow with a long braid and eyes that held a hint of silver sharpness. The woman from my visions, holding a round seed cupped in one hand.

Ice crept into the air. "You should not be here." The ground trembled at Rhianne's quiet, jagged words. "You should be safe."

I knew who Rhianne most wished to keep safe. "But that's impossible," I said, knowing I couldn't fight them both.

The woman gave me a measuring look, as if she heard more than my words. Her mouth quirked into a wry smile. "What is impossible, Summoner?"

"You're Mirinda." Rhianne's daughter, the speaker for whom Rhianne had sent her roots into the gray.

"Indeed." She followed my gaze to the seed she carried. "You are not the only one who can hold to a seed, Liza. I have kept this one for many years. But I owe you an apology. I should have come far sooner. As soon as the crumbling became apparent, I began making my way home, but that journey took some time, for your world has become more perilous since the War. I believe we shared the last part of that journey."

"It was you following us." But she was supposed to be dead, ages and ages ago. *In time Mirinda passed from the Realm.* That wasn't the same as being dead. Rhianne had told me Mirinda wasn't in the gray. She'd known, even if her people had forgotten. But was Mirinda here to stop the crumbling, or to help her mother hold on to it?

"I will send you back," Rhianne said.

"I do not think so. I have lived long enough to know the ways of dying quickly." Pain flashed across Mirinda's face. "My body grows cold back in the Realm. A dramatic gesture, and one I fear has upset Liza's companions, but you would not listen when I sought to speak with you from the living world. You have never listened, not when I first told you these gifts were not right, not when I return this day to tell you again."

A gust rippled through the gray. "It is your presence here that is not right," Rhianne said.

"Yet here I am." Mirinda looked up the length of Rhianne's roots, toward her trunk, then shook her head, as if the story written there were too difficult to read. "Will you listen now, if I tell you the grief your gifts have caused? Of how they made our Realm pull apart from the larger world, and drained power from that world as well—drained away the magic that belongs to every living person by right? Of how they caused our people to forget that any but us had ever held magic, and so led us to use our power to control all those we met from that larger world?"

Mirinda no more approved of her mother's gifts than humans did. Could she make Rhianne let go, where I could not? My mother had so rarely listened to me. "I could not stop all the ways our people misused power," Mirinda said, "and you would not stop them, so I left the Realm at last, determined at least not to aid them. But meetings of our Realm and the World continued to bring pain, until at last the War came, and we all paid the price of your gifts."

"Our worlds were once the same," I said. "Our people were the same."

"Yes." Mirinda bowed her head, as if the thought brought sorrow.

"Your people," I whispered. "My people." All my life, I'd been raised to know how different they were.

"Liza's people were not blameless during the burning," Rhianne said.

"No," Mirinda agreed. "I have traveled their world long enough to know they are quite capable of starting wars even without us. But the price of this War is too high. It has to end, before nothing remains of World or Realm."

"I saved you." Rhianne's voice was a whisper of wind. "You were the one thing I saved, after all the ways in which I failed."

"It was not rescue I sought," Mirinda whispered, just as soft. "It was never to have lost you. I accepted long ago that I could not have that wish. So now you cannot have yours, either." She looked to the shadows drifting around us. "This is over. It has been over a very long time. Let them go."

"It is not over," Rhianne said, and I heard in her the same pride I heard in all her folk. "If you choose to squander the gifts I have offered, others may yet make use of them. So long as our people live beneath the sun, I will keep death from them."

"I'll not allow you to condemn us, Mother." Mirinda's voice turned softer still. *"Go, Rhianne. Seek sleep, seek comfort, seek rest."* The gray shuddered, letting a flash of green through.

The shadows of the dead brushed against me like trickles of snowmelt. "You have less power than you think," Rhianne said. *"Come here, Mirinda."* I felt Rhianne's magic release me as she turned it to calling her daughter.

Mirinda took a step toward her mother. Stopped. Tension crackled in the air between them, like river ice in spring. Green flickered in and out. We needed the green. We had always needed the green.

Rhianne and Mirinda kept calling to each other, calling with their magic, neither moving the other. Rhianne wasn't paying any attention to me, not now. I slipped among the First Tree's roots, into the hollows where the dead's shadows were thickest, knowing moving away from the tree would draw more attention, knowing from a lifetime of practice how much depended on not being seen. I crouched and took my seed in my hands. Rhianne had stopped me from calling a seed once before. Maybe that meant there was power in calling one.

"Grow!" The seed shuddered, and a crack broke its

surface. A thin gray sprout pushed through that crack. Gray was not enough. *"Grow!"*

"Liza! Silence!"

My voice froze inside me, and I choked on my longing for the green.

A hand gripped my shoulder, warm as nothing here was. I looked up. Mirinda looked down at me. Her smile was sadder now. Something flowed from her to me, something that shimmered green-gold in this land without color, filling me with power as rain fills dry earth.

"Go on, Summoner. Make this right."

Magic. Mirinda was lending me her magic, adding it to my own. There was no time to wonder at so great a gift. With all that power behind me, I was stronger than Rhianne after all, strong enough to force my voice out into the gray. *"Grow!"* Something in the seed sparked and caught. *"Seek sky, seek sun, seek life!"* The gray in the seedling gave way to spring green.

"Stop! Seek silence, seek stillness, seek sleep!" Rhianne's anger shook the land, but the seed grew on. The sprout hit a root, and it began branching, sending seeking green threads to wrap around that root, then another, and another, forming a web of green growth.

"Go away, Mirinda!" Rhianne screamed. *"Disturb my work here no more!"*

"And where shall I go, Mother?" With her magic

gone, Mirinda's voice was a small thing, no power in it. "You cannot send me back to life. You can only let me pass beyond the gray. Will you?"

"Grow!" My own voice was strong and clear, magic burning my throat. So much magic, more than any one person was meant to hold. The seedling grew, its web of green grasping at roots, pulling at them. Its shell split in my hand. The flickers of green in the air grew brighter, but Rhianne's roots held firm. *"Grow!"* I called again, and again, and again. The words tore through me as they spilled into the air. The seed shrank, as seeds did when they fed growing things. Something in me faded. My name. I'd have no way of holding my name once the seed was gone.

I faltered at that, and the green web stopped its growth. To let go my name—I would truly be lost then, no hope of returning to life, no promises of what would happen when I passed beyond the gray.

"You feel it, too." No magic in Rhianne's voice now. "You are a summoner. You no more want to let go than I do."

I'd already let go of so much: my father's approval. The hope that my mother could protect me. My sister—my first sister—who I could not protect in turn. Knowing whose fault the War was. Thinking my people free of blame.

There was sorrow in Mirinda's gaze, as if she heard

all I hadn't spoken aloud. She seemed fainter without her magic, like a weaving worn through. Her mother had done so much, too much, to protect her, but Rhianne had failed, too, in the end. It wasn't right.

And nothing any of us could do would change it. The past was like fear. I could not let it control me. People failed me. I failed them. Knowing this, we kept fixing what we could. Sometimes by holding on. Sometimes—by letting go.

I drew my hands apart, and I released the last sliver of seed I held. *"Grow!"*

My name slipped from me as surely as the seed did. My shadow blurred and let go its shape, leaving behind only the faintest memory of who I'd been. The green web grew strong, pulling at the roots all around it. The flickers of green in the air lasted longer.

The web wrenched the roots it held free at last. A stiff, icy wind gusted through the air, and the tree began to topple. I could not move. I could only let that wind blow me and the other shadows from beneath the flailing roots.

High above, branches snapped and fell. Mirinda stepped aside, her hands outstretched. "Come here, Mother," she said, and though her magic was gone, as the First Tree hit the ground, her mother's shadow slid free.

Rhianne seemed old, bent with age like no faerie folk

I'd ever seen. She looked at the tree, at the gray and its shadows, at her daughter's shadow last of all. I saw fear, regret, pain—I no longer remembered what those things felt like.

Mirinda reached for her mother. "Shall we see what lies beyond this place?"

Rhianne's shoulders hunched further, as if beneath some great burden, but she took her daughter's hand and whispered, "Go."

Another gust tossed me farther from them, lightly as a toy. "Thank you, Liza," the younger woman whispered, but I didn't know who she spoke to, or why. There was a moment's fear, and then the wind took that, too. I flew on its dancing current, through a field that kept flickering: gray-green, green-gray. Laughter rippled through me. Letting go was all right after all. The wind blew me away, toward whatever it was that came next, and I couldn't remember why I'd wanted to stop it. My shadow began to unravel, threads pulling apart, and that was right, too.

Until one of those threads caught on something, stopping me with a painful lurch. A tree. Not Rhianne's tree, but another tree, one that called to something deep inside me. I wanted to fight it, only I couldn't remember how. I was finished. I was ready. I'd let go.

Yet the new tree pulled on me, knew me. "Liza," it said.

Or maybe that was the man whose shadow stood beside the tree. I knew him as surely as I knew the tree itself—a tree I'd planted, a tree whose roots had always stretched beyond the gray. "Caleb," I whispered. There was pain in his name. I was supposed to be done with pain.

"There is not much time." He carried something, something that also held a whisper of green. "Tell me, Liza. Do you want to go back?"

"Back?" It took me a moment to work out what he meant. Back home, to the crumbling world where people held to each other, and failed to hold to each other; where all things wound down in the end. The laughter left me. In the world, there were small things to set right every day, instead of this one large thing I knew I'd done right once and for all.

In the world, more than this tree and Caleb knew my name.

I felt my shadow taking on shape once more, a rough shape like a child's smudged charcoal drawing. "I don't know if I want to go back."

"Will you trust me, then, to know you well enough to choose for you?"

Did I trust him? I couldn't remember. I thought maybe sometimes I did. "All right," I said.

"Come, then." His cold shadow hand took hold of

mine. He stepped into the tree, and I followed, scraps of memory returning. I'd trusted him before, with more lives than mine, but I couldn't puzzle out whether he'd been worthy of that trust.

Green threads flared bright around me. "Our paths lie in different directions from here," Caleb said. "Perhaps we will meet again, beyond the gray or—sooner." He gave me a small, sad smile. "All may yet be well, Liza. Tell your sister—"

But I never found out what he wanted me to tell her, because with a lurch the green gave way. There was time to grab a handful of threads in my hand, and then with a shudder, flesh and stone closed around my shadow like a scab over an old wound, and ice raised goose bumps on my human skin.

A new voice spoke my name, and I knew him, too, as surely as he knew me. "Liza," he said, over and over again.

There was no magic in his call, but it did not matter. I held to that voice like a lantern in fog, until at last I found the strength to open my eyes.

"Matthew," I said.

⌐ *Chapter 20* ⌐

He looked down at me, face streaked with ash, mouth open. It took me a moment to realize that he was sitting on the ground and my body was draped over his arms. I reached up with my good hand and felt tears on his cheek. I brought my fingers to my lips, tasting their saltiness. "I'm Liza," I said, feeling the name settle firmly back beneath my skin.

"Yes," Matthew said. I sat up, and he helped me to my feet.

"Good of you to come back," Elin said dryly.

Matthew wrapped his arms around me. I inhaled a breath of cold, stale air. The smell didn't seem as strong as before, but I looked around and saw we stood in a small island of life, a few scant yards across, darkness pressing in from all sides. The standing stone was gone. I wasn't home yet.

Tolven crouched beside his tree, rocking back and forth, chanting under his breath, "Green, green, green." Beyond him and Elin, at the base of the First Tree's stump, a woman lay motionless on the ground, arms outstretched, throat slit. *Mirinda.* Crimson blood stained her face and hands and soaked her dress, broken by a scattering of silver dust beneath the chain she wore. The colors seemed thin and pale as all the remaining world around us, as if color were an illusion—save for something bright that pulsed in my stone hand. I looked down and saw green threads, the threads I'd grabbed from the gray. Could the others see them, too?

"So my grandmother was right, and the world winds down at last." Elin lifted her head, facing that ending as surely as I'd faced the gray.

Sound seemed as muted as sight. "Nothing's winding down." I looked from Mirinda to the First Tree's stump. It held no shadow now. "The world—everything's all right now." Mirinda's power had left me, and my voice was hoarse, as if I'd used too much of it in the gray.

"Your world, perhaps," Elin said. "But that does us little good here. If anything remains of the Realm beyond this small space where we stand, I know no way to reach it."

"The dark isn't moving any closer," Matthew said, holding me still. "That's something."

"It is not enough," Elin said. "Not when our most basic powers fail us, sight and sound losing their very sharpness."

Those gifts included not only long life, but night vision, and distance hearing, and silent walking, and all the ways in which we are both harder to hurt and harder to heal. Sound, sight, smell—they weren't only muted by the darkness pressing in on us. They'd dulled because Rhianne's gifts had left us at last.

Including glamour. I turned in Matthew's hold, grabbed his head with my good hand, and drew him toward me, kissing him hard and fast, feeling his lips warm against mine. We pulled apart, breathless, and I looked into his eyes. They were bright, but there was no hint of glamour there. He traced a finger along my lips. I hadn't told him to do that. I hadn't even wished it, though once he did it, it was exactly what I wanted.

"It really is all right," I said, and Matthew nodded.

"You two have the strangest idea of what all right looks like." Elin stared into the dark. Silver threads streaked the emptiness.

I looked at the green threads in my stone hand, and I reached my flesh hand toward that dark. *Come here.* The call scraped my throat like broken glass, but silver threads flowed into my outstretched hand. Icy threads, numbing my fingers—I drew my hands together, and the green threads' warmth made the silver easier to bear. I held both hands out to Elin, offering her silver threads from the world, green threads from someplace beyond the world. "Can you weave these into something that will lead us through the dark?"

Fear and hope flashed across Elin's face, making her seem terribly young. "I can surely try." She plunged her hands into the light I held, and it wrapped around her wrists and fingers, flowing from me to her. She brought her hands together, and the strands tangled like unspun wool. She ran her fingers through them. Breath by breath, the shimmering fibers aligned themselves, silver and green, warp and weft.

The chill faded from the air. Rough fibers turned into a slowly brightening weaving as Elin pulled row after shining row tight. Matthew's eyes seemed huge by its light. Elin held the weaving out toward the dark as she worked. The darkness retreated as that weaving grew, as surely as it had at the crossroads. The open space around us grew as well, but there was still no clear way through the dark beyond it, and the unwoven fibers in Elin's hands were running out.

"*Come here!*" I carded more silver out of the dark

and passed it to her. Her weaving grew thinner, weaker. She needed more green as well.

. Tolven stumbled to his feet. "The tree!" he cried.

I looked at his tree, felt the green life within it. *"Come here!"* That life flowed toward me like an unfurling seed, turning to thread in my hand. I gave that to Elin, too. *"Come here!"* Every call sent pain stabbing through my throat, but I did not stop. I called all the light I could, silver and green, and passed it to Elin. The pain spread, and my legs threatened to give way, but I felt Matthew's hands on my shoulders, steadying me. I leaned against him as I fed Elin bright threads that thrummed with life and power. Sweat trickled down my neck. When had the air grown so warm?

"Come here!" Tolven's tree came undone as I called, strand by green strand. Elin wove with fierce intensity, her face wild by the light. Her weaving shimmered and danced as she cast it out into the dark, danced the way my shadow had danced when it flew through the gray.

The green in Tolven's tree ran out, and he fell wailing to the ground as trunk and branches crumbled to gray, but there seemed no end to the silver I called. *"Come here."* The dark retreated further, letting in something new: blue sky, yellow sun, brown earth. I called those colors to me, too, felt their life and light as well, and knew they came not from Faerie, but from my own bright world. The land around us blurred, and the dust of Faerie fell away as I drew that place of life and light to us. Elin's hands faltered, as if she realized what I did—that we weren't saving Faerie but abandoning it—and then she turned to the work with new intensity.

I kept calling the things of my world to us—bright things, shining things, broken things—and Elin accepted them, weaving the last threads of her dying world in among them. My voice faded to a burning whisper. Elin's weaving found its way to a river—the River—and darkness rolled away, leaving behind blue-green waters beneath a high sun, waters that flowed south with nothing of death in their voice. Faerie was gone. This weaving was for my world, the human world, a flawed thing filled with crumbling holes into which Elin wove her bright cloth. The shimmering threads stretched farther and farther, out into that world, threading their way into earth and sky, rivers and stars. Seasons flowed, one into another. Time lost meaning, became one more thread I gave Elin to weave. Something sparked, and the weaving caught life, spreading by its own power into all the places Elin couldn't reach. Shining threads slipped from her fingers, and her eyes reflected their light. Bright light, so bright that in it I saw—

Karin and Allie and Nys, leading the faerie folk through the forest, winding their way around the crumbling and the dark, stopping at the top of a hill to look back as all the silver brightness drained from the Arch, leaving behind dull tarnished metal, even as another light, a brighter light, found its way into the very fabric of the world—

Allie, an older Allie, her hair more clear than red, walking a winter path from town to town, another girl from her town—Kimi, a plant speaker with green vines wrapped around her arms and neck—by her side—

Karin standing by the Wall that had protected that town for so long, only something had changed, making it seem no more than a tangle of overgrown weeds, no magic left in it. "The Wall has served its purpose," Karin said. "It is time for us all to learn to live without it—"

The oldest Afters from my town, Hope and Seth and Charlotte, standing before my town's Council. "They're not going," Hope said. "Not Ethan, not Tara, not Tara's daughter, not my son. You will live with our magic, or you will live without us all—"

Myself, heading into a winter forest to find Matthew—

Matthew, heading into an autumn forest to find me—

Home, I thought. *I want to go home.* Caleb had chosen right, after all. I wanted to live in this bright, broken world as long as I could.

The visions faded. Matthew's hand slipped into mine, and I wrapped my fingers around his.

"It is done." Elin's eyes remained bright.

Beside her, Tolven struggled to his feet. "This is the human world?"

"It is," Matthew said.

"It seems a good place," Tolven told him solemnly.

Shapes came clear. Blue sky. Red leaves. A sloped hillside, on which we stood. A tree—an autumn tree, a living quia tree—upon it, just a few paces away from us, leaves burning with autumn fire. That tree knew me, and I knew it, as surely as I knew, deep down, that its roots stretched only into brown earth and the green beyond it, and held nothing more of gray death.

But I did not know the toddler who looked up from beneath the tree, saw me, and burst into startled laughter.

~⁓ *Chapter 21* ⌒

The child ducked her head, suddenly shy, and turned
to look at a second, older child who hid behind the tree.
That child I knew, though he was taller than I remembered: Kyle.

Elin pulled her feather cloak about her. "Everything's
changed," she said.

"The trees are not green." Tolven looked all around.
"But they are well, and whole."

Elin grabbed both his hands. "And so are you," she
whispered.

"And so am I," Tolven agreed, and leaned his head
on her shoulder.

The world seemed so bright, like new-forged steel,
silver threads still shining at the edges of my sight. A leaf
fell from the quia tree and blew toward us. I released

Matthew's hand to catch it, and it did not dissolve to dust. It was an ordinary autumn leaf, no more, no less.

That was when I heard someone else, breathing shallow breaths, watching us. I turned. *Mom.* I could not seem to speak.

"Tara," Matthew said.

Mom didn't move. She stared at us, while behind her the sky blazed with dusk. The child moved to hide behind her. There'd been no child this age in my town when I'd left.

My stomach did a little flip as suspicion crept into my thoughts. It was Matthew who spoke the suspicion aloud. "How long have we been gone?"

Mom's breathing sped up, and her face paled. "A year. I thought you were—we all thought you were—" I feared she might faint, she looked that stunned.

The baby crept out from behind her, a baby with ordinary brown fuzz on her head and a hint of silver speckling her eyes. I knelt to look at her. "What is your name?" The words burned my throat. I'd called so much.

The child looked down, still shy.

"It's Mirinda." Mom's voice shook. "Rinda for short. We wanted you to name her, but you didn't come back, and Karin—she said it was an old name among the faerie folk, and that it had been out of use long enough to bring it back."

"Mirinda's a good name." My voice was hoarse, used up. I wanted to go to Mom, but I couldn't get my legs to close the distance between us.

"A year," Matthew said, his voice strained. "A whole year. Gram—"

"She's fine," Tara said. "We need to tell her you're here—" But she just kept staring, as if afraid we would disappear if she looked away.

Kyle came out from behind the tree, a butterfly trembling on his fingers and a yellow cat winding around his legs. Mirinda reached for the butterfly, then drew back, as if uncertain.

Kyle saw Elin and stuck out his tongue, saw me and turned swiftly away.

"Kyle?" Was he as angry at me now as a year ago?

Kyle marched up to Matthew, as if he were the one safe person here. "You brought her back," he said.

"We brought each other back." Matthew's gaze took in Elin and Tolven as well as me. "All of us."

Kyle's face scrunched up. He whispered something I couldn't make out. Matthew leaned down, and Kyle repeated it.

"That's not your fault," Matthew said gently.

"Tell her," Kyle said.

Matthew turned to me. "Kyle says he's sorry he got angry and he's sorry he made you run away."

"Kyle." Speaking hurt, but this was too important. "Matthew's right. None of this is your fault."

Kyle stuck out his lower lip, and I knew he didn't believe me. He sniffled. "I'm not angry anymore," he said.

"I know." Throat aching, I looked at Mom. "Neither am I." Mom would stay or she would leave, and I could no more decide for her than for anyone else. I could only find a way to live with what she decided.

"Lizzy—" But Mom couldn't seem to find words to go with that.

Mirinda reached for Kyle's butterfly again. It burst into flame, and the toddler burst into tears. She didn't know yet that some things couldn't last.

Her tears stopped abruptly, as baby tears did. Mirinda looked up, toward the quia tree, tottered forward, and fell. Mom swept her from the ground. Mirinda hung limp in her hold, and my breath caught, but Mom didn't look frightened. "Mirinda!" she called.

"Not again," Kyle sighed.

I followed their gazes and saw a scrap of shadow running circles around the tree. Rinda could control her own shadow, I realized. Just like summoners long ago.

"She always comes back," Mom said. "But it can take a while."

Rinda stopped to put her shadow hands to the bark. She giggled, and then her shadow reached into the tree.

"Mirinda!" I cried, afraid she'd lose herself to that tree, but she stopped, hands in just past the wrists, to look up at us curiously. "Name?" she asked.

Trees had no names, save for the First Tree, which was also Rhianne—but Rhianne was gone, surely she was. I unfocused my gaze and looked at this tree's shadow, looked and looked until my eyes threatened to cramp and at last I saw the fainter shadow within it.

Not Rhianne's shadow. This shadow looked down at Rinda as if he'd never get enough of looking at her. I swallowed hard as I moved to my sister's side. "Caleb." It wasn't only trying to speak that made my throat burn.

He nodded soberly. My legs threatened to give way, and Matthew laid a steadying hand on my shoulder. *Our paths lie in different directions from here,* Caleb had said. He couldn't come back, but he'd come as far as he could.

"Allie told me about Kaylen," Mom said softly. She didn't understand. She knew the name I spoke, not the shadow I saw. I took the coin from around my neck and hung it from a low branch, my eyes on that shadow.

"Should I try to call you out of the tree?" I asked him, but as I spoke, I knew, as Rhianne had not, that sometimes things really were over. Caleb knew it, too; he shook his head, no.

Mom gave a little gasp, and I knew she'd worked it out. She walked toward the tree, slowly, steadily.

"Do you want me to send you on?" I asked Caleb. Again he shook his head, then moved his lips, as if trying to say something. Whatever it was, it was beyond my human hearing.

"Not now," I said. A nod. "Not ever?" Caleb shook his head. "You'll stay for a time?" I asked, and he nodded.

"This is not possible," Elin said, while Tolven simply stared at the tree. Caleb knelt down to squeeze Rinda's shadow hands. Rinda leaned forward to wrap her shadow arms around him, everything but her legs disappearing into the tree.

"Kaylen." Mom couldn't see him, but she set Rinda's body down, and she pressed her hands to the smooth trunk. Caleb stood, Rinda's shadow arms still around his legs, and pressed his hands to Mom's, though neither could push past the bark between them. I brushed my hand across my eyes and found them damp.

"You did what needed doing, Kaylen. I know that." No tears in Mom's voice. She'd had a year to accept this, as I had not. "I'll honor and mourn that all my life. We had one good summer together." Something in her voice caught. "It will have to be enough."

"I'm so sorry," I said, not knowing if I spoke to Mom or to Caleb. "I never meant for this to happen." My own voice broke, and Matthew's arms wrapped tightly around me. "Never."

Caleb held his hands out toward me, but I could no more push through the tree to reach him than Mom could. "Thank you," I whispered instead. "For sending me back."

Caleb nodded, acknowledging that. Rinda's shadow released him. She slipped out of the tree, giggling, and reached up for me. I pulled away from Matthew to lift her shadow into my arms. The shadow was cold, but it was a cold I'd learned to handle long ago.

I have a sister now. The thought seemed strange as the year I had lost. I knelt beside Rinda's body. Caleb watched us, his smile no less real for the sorrow it held. Rinda's shadow slipped from my arms to settle back beneath her skin. Her whole body shook with more giggles as she toddled to her feet.

I laughed, too, only it turned into a sob, and then somehow we were all holding each other, my mother and my sister and me, one giant crying hug that seemed to go on forever. Mom pulled Kyle and Matthew in, and Kyle's cat pulled itself in, climbing up the back of my pants leg with needle-sharp claws. Only Elin and Tolven remained apart, silent.

When we pulled away from one another at last, Elin asked stiffly, "Tell me, Tara. Have you had any word of our people?"

Mom nodded. "They're doing all right. Winter was hard on them, but it was hard on us all, and they made it through. If they sometimes make for uncomfortable neighbors, well, that would hardly be the greatest challenge we've faced since the War." She laughed uneasily. "Though some in this town would argue that."

"Neighbors?" Elin said.

"Clayburn," Mom told her. "They had to go somewhere, and with winter coming, there wasn't much time to choose. And there were houses there that could be rebuilt, and some rations already in storage." Mom gave Elin a hard look, a measuring look.

"Yes," Elin said sharply. "I am well aware of these things." Clayburn was the town she'd destroyed.

"What about Allie?" I said. "And Karin?"

"Both fine. They've gone home to Washville, though Allie spends a lot of time in Clayburn now. Karin, too." Mom smiled then. "The world might have been ending, but Allie made it here in time to see to Rinda's birth, though she has both her town and what remains of Faerie to look after now."

Dusk was fading, taking the color with it. Elin turned to Tolven. "We should go. It's a long walk to Clayburn." She sounded wearier than I'd ever heard her.

Tolven looked to me. "By the bonds between us, Liza, might we find a resting place here tonight?"

"We do not need their help," Elin said.

"Even so, you could hardly be blamed for wanting

rest before facing the Court and all its politics." Mom laughed again, and something in her relaxed. "You're both welcome to stay the night, Elin."

"You would risk that?" Elin said. "After all I have done?"

"Would our town allow it?" I asked, not sure, for a moment, whether I wanted them to or not.

"I'll not ask permission to invite guests into my own house." The steel in Mom's voice surprised me.

"In that case," Elin said softly, "it would be an honor to accept."

I looked at Elin, and she looked at me, and something passed between us. "If the world ever needs saving again," she said solemnly, "I shall remember to seek you out, Liza."

"And I you," I said, knowing the words for the sacred vow they were.

Kyle knelt in the dirt, digging; the cat had crawled onto his head. Mirinda sidled up beside me, reaching for my stone hand as tentatively as she'd reached for the butterfly. Her fingers wrapped around it, and then the shadow of her hand moved beyond her skin and through my stone. It was easy, feeling her shadow fingers so clearly in mine, to tighten my hold on her in turn, and as my shadow hand moved, my stone hand moved with it, and I knew it truly wasn't dead after all.

The light was nearly gone, but the night seemed to glow silver still. Kyle stood, both his hands covered with ladybugs, and looked right at me. "Home," he said, and it was clearly an order.

I laughed, and then I was crying all over again. "Home," I agreed.

Matthew reached for my free hand, but Kyle grabbed it first, and ladybugs crawled between our palms. Matthew shrugged and took Kyle's hand instead, while Caleb kept watching us all. Rinda waved shyly at him. She would know him, and he would know her, at least this little bit.

We walked down the hillside together, Mirinda's shadow hand in mine, all of us matching our pace to her toddling steps, until at last she demanded I carry her. Kyle's ladybugs crawled from my hand into her hair. She laughed again. She liked to laugh, I could tell.

I suddenly wanted more than anything to keep her safe enough that she'd always laugh without fear, wanted it so badly it made my chest hurt.

Beyond the hillside, wilder trees lined the path, and their shadows reached for us as we walked. I couldn't know about always, only about right now. So right now I used my magic to keep the shadows away—to keep those I cared about safe—all the way home.

~⊃ *Chapter 22* ⊂~

Green buds were everywhere as Allie and Matthew and
I reached the outskirts of Clayburn. Spring was coming
on its own this year, a change as gradual as autumn's
coming had been. Mom said it had been so last year
as well, but I hadn't been here, so all through the day's
walk, I'd marveled at how much more slowly and shyly
spring arrived when no magic compelled it, until Allie
said, "That's what you get for being gone so long." Last
fall I'd thought she would never forgive us for letting her
think we were dead a whole year, as if we had done it
on purpose.

The black dust was gone from the paths between
towns, or else melted with winter's snow into the soil.
The faerie folk had rebuilt most of Clayburn's houses,
with strange round angles only those accustomed to

building with magic would think to use, but a few remained burned and broken, because Elin had insisted, when she returned, on that reminder of those who had died here.

That she'd gotten her people to agree was a sign that they would accept her power, but not so great a sign as tonight would be.

Karin met us at the edge of the town, dressed in a scuffed brown leather vest and pants, a quia leaf pattern embroidered with green thread beneath one shoulder. I'd only seen those clothes in visions: they were the clothes Karinna the Fierce had worn into battle. A circlet of hawthorn and ivy was wrapped around her loose hair, and a long knife hung at her side.

"I'm glad you could come," she said, and her smile was not fierce at all. It was the smile of the woman who'd let Matthew and me into her town when we'd needed rescue, though she hadn't known whether we could be trusted. "You are well?"

"Yes," I said, my voice hoarse. Allie had done what she could for it, but it had never returned entirely. "Rinda's fine, too." Karin visited her niece as often as she could. "And Elin?" I asked.

"A part of her yet wishes I would change my mind, and a part of me does not blame her," Karin said. "We have talked much these past weeks."

"I'm glad." I'd been talking a lot with my mother, too, though I suspected those talks were easier. Mom had decided to stay after all. She said she'd realized it wasn't only Rinda who mattered, but all of the other Afters, and also that if her daughter could help weave an entire world back together, maybe she could find courage enough to help look after a single town.

Her staff in hand, Karin led us to a house near the edge of Clayburn, where we changed out of our travel clothes. I put on leather pants and a sweater and the owl-feather cloak Elin had gifted me, and I pulled my hair, which had gone completely clear in the gray, back from my face. I slung my bow and arrow in their cases over my shoulders and sheathed my knife at my belt. Karin had told me it was fitting that I be seen as the warrior and hunter I was. I still hadn't the skill I once had, but as I gained more control over my stone hand, my arrows flew closer to true.

Allie wore a long white coat over her jeans—it had belonged to her mother, who'd been training to be a doctor, Before—along with the medical kit Caleb had given her when she'd come into her magic, so that she could be known as the healer she was. Elin's gift to Allie was inside: bandages that did not require knots to hold themselves firmly in place.

Matthew wore his deerskin pants and jacket and said

he didn't need to be known as anything but Matthew. He didn't have any gifts from Elin, because only those who'd eaten of the quia seeds, or who were descended from those who had, were supposed to be invited to this ceremony. It had never occurred to those who'd decided that that the seeds might one day lose their power, or that those who ate them might include humans. Elin had said that if I chose to bring my consort with me, it certainly wasn't her place to refuse, which was her way of inviting Matthew without breaking any rules.

Karin had to leave before us, but she and Elin had food sent, a stew of old carrots and dried goat jerky that held none of the rotten sweetness of the meals we'd eaten in Faerie. One of our gifts to Elin had been crop seeds from both my and Allie's towns, which would help make next winter less hungry for Clayburn than this one.

Nys came, well past sunset, to lead Allie, Matthew, and me to an open clearing, lit by a full silver moon above and by hundreds of green and yellow fireflies around us, coaxed to life out of season. Beyond the clearing, a spring river flowed swift and loud at the base of limestone bluffs.

At the clearing's center, Karin sat on a chair made from the same limestone, living vines and carved leaves both adorning it. Elin knelt at her feet, her hair pulled back in a silver butterfly clasp. The weaver wore a long green and silver dress, bright colors that echoed the threads woven into the world around us. I could still see those threads of magic and light, in stray moments when I'd almost forgotten to look for them, and I knew Elin could, too.

Nys left us a few paces from the throne, for that's what it was. "It is good to see you well," he told me before slipping away, but there was no warmth in his words. We were not friends, any more than he and Elin were. It was Elin who would have to work with him, though.

Tolven slipped into place beside us with an easy smile, his tunic and pants the same colors as Elin's dress. Other faerie folk entered the clearing around us, silent as gathering humans rarely were, save for the sound of their steps against the soft earth. Tolven stood near the throne for many reasons, but I suspected one was as protection, because any fey who mistrusted the three humans in their town would nonetheless hesitate to offend Tolven, whose magic had kept them alive since the War.

Some of the faerie folk stumbled and had to be supported by others. Fire fever still lingered among them, but slowly, carefully, Allie was doing what she could to heal it.

Once the clearing was full, Karin lifted her head to the sky and sang, the same wordless song Elin had sung for Caleb, only now there was no sadness in it. The sounds were not sounds human voices could make—the faerie folk had their mysteries still—but Allie hummed along. After a moment, so did Matthew and I, though my rough voice marred the perfect notes.

Surrounded by that song, Karin drew Elin to her feet, then felt for the arm of the throne to give her daughter two things: a shining black stone from Faerie, streaked with silver, which Nys had granted to Karin in another, more rushed ceremony performed on a forest trail, one in which Karin had officially taken her mother's place as heir; and a bright green quia leaf from a descendant of the First Tree, which I'd granted Karin with no ceremony at all when she last visited and which she'd kept alive with her magic ever since. Elin accepted them both. Karin opened her mouth to speak, but before she could, a spark that held the faintest echo of stone and leaf leaped from her to Elin.

Tolven laughed. "It appears the magic is more eager than the pace of the ceremony that accompanies it," he said.

Elin's eyes grew wide. "The Realm is not gone," she whispered. "I can feel it all around us, in the very fabric of this human world."

"Yes," Karin said soberly. "That weaving was well done, Daughter. You and Liza have brought our two worlds back together, as they were always meant to be. And now the Realm is truly yours, for I hear its voice no longer." Karin lifted the circlet from her head, and for the first time, her steady hands fumbled.

Elin helped her mother set the circlet in place on her own head. "It is all right," Elin said softly, as if believing it for the first time. "Everything's going to be all right."

Karin raised her voice and said, loud enough for those at the farthest edges of the clearing to hear, "I hereby relinquish all claim on the Realm and its people to my daughter, who has been with you through the fire and the crumbling, as I have not. See to it that you are worthy of the gifts she brings you." Karin stood, and Elin grabbed her mother into a hug that I suspected was not part of the ceremony at all.

There were cheers after that, and Elin took her place on the throne. Tolven led Karin back to us before taking his place at Elin's side, as was appropriate for a queen's consort. He and Elin exchanged the briefest of smiles before Elin turned to the faerie folk who lined up to approach her throne and give the oath she demanded of them, as was now her right.

Nys approached Elin first, and I was close enough to hear him say, "I do this for Kaylen more than you. You will not find me an easy ally."

"I am well aware of that," Elin said. "I welcome your oath just the same, and your help in the years ahead."

So Nys repeated the words Elin had chosen, words that had never before been spoken to a ruler of Faerie by her subjects:

> *Blessed are the powers that grant me*
> *magic.*
> *I promise to use their gift well.*
> *To help mend my world,*
> *To help mend all worlds.*
> *And should I forget to mend,*
> *Should I refuse to mend,*
> *Still I will remember*
> *To do no harm.*

It took a long time for all the faerie folk to give their oaths, some more willingly than others. It would be no small task for Elin to lead them. I understood, from Mom and from Karin, that the ways of the Faerie Court were more winding and complex than those of any town Council.

Tolven gave his oath last, as was also fitting for a consort. Only Allie and Matthew and I gave no oath at all, for we were here not as Elin's subjects, but as ambassadors from our towns. Mirinda could give Elin her oath one day, if she chose, but for now, we were doing our best to keep both my sister and mother from the notice of as much of Elin's town as possible. Elin had pledged her help in this, because Mirinda was her cousin, and because Elin was safer, too, the fewer people who knew she wasn't the last of her line.

Once Tolven's oath was given, there was dancing, and music, and wine far stronger than what Nys had served Allie and me in Faerie, until at last the sun rose and the fireflies flickered out.

After that, and after a day's rest, we went home, Karin and Allie to their town, Matthew and me to ours, with promises to visit each other once the crops were planted. Matthew and I took as much care with the journey back as the journey there, because spring still had its dangers, and the trees were already awake enough to seek our blood. But some things had changed: last winter, no human shadows had walked among the sleeping trees, and in all seasons the dead now found rest without my help.

Karin hopes their shadows might find something after all, beyond the gray, something more than a simple ending, but there is no way to know. She says we will all just have to face that when our time comes. She smiles when she says it, and the smile brings out the faintest hint of wrinkles at the corners of her mouth, as sure a sign as any that Rhianne's gifts are gone. Yet if Karin fears the dark that now lies ahead of us all, she gives no sign. She is still Karinna the Fierce, after all.

For I have seen that far-off day, and I know she will face it with grace. I see so much more, now that the world is going to endure. I see Allie grown up, still walking among our three towns but traveling farther, too, finding other healers and training them. I see Kyle, nearly grown as well, a hunting cat at his side. I see Elin and Tolven and Nys, struggling to help their people, sometimes together, sometimes at odds with one another. I see my mother, crying when she thinks I can't hear, but I see her older, too, with gray in her hair, taking up the flute she hasn't played since the War and smiling more readily than she does now. I see my sister, growing older as well, laughing, always laughing, even as she gains better control over her shadow. I see Matthew—but I'll share all I've seen of Matthew with none but him, save to say that it brings me far more joy than sorrow.

Matthew and I visited the quia tree on our way home from Clayburn, to share the ceremony with Caleb. Mom talked to his tree sometimes, too, and Allie and Karin when they visited, and it was all we could do to keep Rinda and Kyle from playing there endlessly.

As Matthew and I climbed the hillside, I felt the tree's familiar green presence, and Caleb's presence, and an echo of something more that I hadn't felt since a long-ago day when we feared the world might be crumbling away.

I nodded at Caleb as I stepped beneath his tree, as even those who couldn't see or sense him had begun to do, and I looked up into the tree's branches. They were heavy with green seeds. Ordinary seeds that pulled on me with the same faint green all seeds held, nothing stronger. I reached for one, and it came free in my hand. There was no magic in it, and it would not protect me from anything. That was all right. Protection was not all seeds were for. From within the tree, Caleb nodded back at me, as if he knew it, too.

I found a flat clear spot, near the tree but not too near. Matthew helped me dig, and I buried the seed beneath the soil. When we were done, I took Matthew's face in my hands, stone and flesh shaping themselves to his skin. I brushed my lips against his, just for a moment. His lips strayed to my hair, and the moment went on longer than either of us intended, but at last I turned back to where the seed lay buried.

My voice was hoarse and battered, but it was yet strong. I put my magic into it, and I reached for the green that came from a place none of us fully understood.

And I called to it, *"Grow."*

⌒ACKNOWLEDGMENTS ⌒

Many thanks to: C. S. Adler, Barbara Bloom, Dawn Dixon, Kathleen Duey, Larry Hammer, Jill Knowles, Vicky Loebel, Patricia McCord, and Jennifer J. Stewart for reading all or part of the manuscript. Jo Walton for giving me Nysraneth's name. Larry and Jennifer again, for rereading as often as needed, usually on short notice. My editor, Jim Thomas, who's done so much to help shape Liza's character from the start. Chelsea Eberly, Courtney Carbone, Heather Palisi, Ellice Lee, Dominique Cimina, Emily Meyer, and everyone else at Random House who's helped see *Faerie After* out into the world. My agent, Nancy Gallt, her assistant, Marietta Zacker, and foreign rights agent Ellen Greenberg. All the booksellers, librarians, bloggers, and especially readers who've become a part of Liza's journey. I feel like I've never found the right words to say how very much I appreciate you, but I truly do. Liza's been a part of my own writing journey, one way or another, for most of my career, and it's an honor and a delight to share that journey with you all.

J a n n i L e e S i m n e r

lives in the Arizona desert, where the plants know how to bite and even the dandelions have thorns. In spite of these things—or perhaps because of them—she's convinced she lives in one of the most stunning places on Earth. Janni has written the three books of the Bones of Faerie Trilogy—*Bones of Faerie, Faerie Winter,* and *Faerie After*—as well as a contemporary Icelandic fantasy, *Thief Eyes.* She's also published four books for younger readers and more than thirty short stories, including one in the *Welcome to Bordertown* anthology.